# Son of the Wind

# Son of the Wind

## Sequel to... The Story of Ganador

## Norma Grimes

Published by Norma Grimes.
Apartado 1078
Sucursal 1
Estepona 29680
Malaga
Spain

SON OF THE WIND

IBSN 978-84-617-4587-6

Book formatted by www.bookformatting.co.uk.

# Contents

# Acknowledgements

I would like to thank the following, without whose help it would not have been possible to write this book: Geoff, Samantha, Family, Fernando d'Andrade, Family, Manuel Sabino Duarte, Val Thornber, Sue Atkins, All my friends at Estepona Writer's Group, Vetequin Estepona, Kit Rushton and N Jimenez.

Literature

The Spanish Horse ... Fernando d'Andrade
Xenophon ... works of

To my family, with love

Also by Norma Grimes

The Story of Ganador

Son of the Wind

# About The Author

Norma is a musician and writer on classical equitation. She lives in Andalucia with husband Geoff and daughter Samantha, close to her passion, Iberian horses. Norma studied classical riding in Portugal and Vienna and is an associate of the Royal College London, Licentiate of the Royal Academy and has taught in colleges within the U.K.

This is the story of Ganador V, Spanish State Stallion – believed to be the first Pure Spanish Stallion to walk on English soil since the Reign of Charles 11. In ancient times combat horses bred in South Western Iberia were amazing for their speed and bravery; some say they were bred by the wind.

*'One does not see the wind, and the marvel of the wind can perform many wonders.' Aristotle.*

**Over the valley' Toby Jug Farm, 1980**

# Prologue.

# Son of the Wind

*Toby Jug Farm and Stables, Moonraker Heights, Yorkshire Moors*

Toby Jug Farm and stables stood almost on the very edge of the moors, high above the old mill towns of Todmorden and Hebden Bridge. Built in the early seventeenth century, the farm had hand carved mullioned windows, huge stone fireplaces and breathtaking views over the valley.

There was a scattering of maybe twenty farms; some on the moorland side of the road, others on the valley side that swept to the front of the farm. Nearly all the other farms and cottages in this remote area were strung out along the narrow moorland road, accessible only by rough, deeply rutted soil tracks that climbed over the horizon to the uninhabited spread of open moors.

The inner stretch of moor was remote and unfriendly; a place where it was usually raining and cold, with a threat of a storm never far away, the howling of a wind somewhere in the distance. Local sheep farmers called the open moors 'the ocean'- a place to keep well away from with its many bogs, sudden storms and freezing winds.

The farm stood in two differing worlds. To the back existed a wilderness of open moors, and to the front was a valley, a very beautiful valley with three semi moorland fields sloping gently downwards towards a more sheltered area, where banks and hills formed a barrier to freezing winds and blizzards.

At the place where the sloping pasture fell away and became

flat, stood a rich green meadow where mountain hares ran free, and a sparkling stream meandered down to the river that flowed through the gorge.

Four, dry-stone walls sheltered the meadow from cruel moorland winds and lashing rain, a fact that allowed a tapestry of delicate wild flowers and grasses to survive and flourish within the protection of these sturdy ramparts. I called this charming meadow, 'the hare run,' as not a day went by without seeing these creatures in the shadow of its walls or playing by the stream.

In the hollow of the valley, was a cavernous, rocky gorge, where mountain birds sheltered in winter, and in spring the call of a cuckoo echoed hauntingly across the farmland, always before six a.m. A sound so intoxicating, that I sometimes woke before this hour, knowing it would soon be gone.

A fast running river flowed through the foot of the gorge, with green fertile sides. Moisture from the river filled its banks with ferns, mosses and wild rhododendron bushes, which stood as high as the few half dead trees.

In the distance, loomed the hills and crags of North Yorkshire, towering over the farmland … shading the pasture with a haze of gold then lavender light through the months of spring and summer. I could never resist watching the phenomenon of light and cloud flooding into the valley, the allure of its endless detail. The miracle of nature coming round once more...

At the top of the track was a narrow moorland road which served as a link between the counties of Lancashire and Yorkshire, once important as a stagecoach route and the travel of wealthy passengers en route between Scotland and Lancaster. Local's referred to the moorland road as, 'King's Causeway,' an old name they said, that told you everything you needed to know about its history.

If you look very closely, you will find the meeting of two worlds on the moorland road. On the north side of the road, and as far as the eye can see was a world of open moors, bleak and abandoned. To the south and sheer at the roadside plunged a world of valleys and gorges, of rivers and hills. I never tired of gazing down into these deep-set valleys from my high farmstead … watching colors change through the seasons, finding new paths to explore or hidden rivers to ride across … and always in the distance endless pictures passing before my eyes, until forty years later I can dissect each one, as if the images happened yesterday…

Along the moorland road stood the 17C Shepherds Rest Inn, a place where every stone, flag and cobble held secrets of times long ago. An important place within the hamlet of Moonraker Heights, the only place to meet others or listen to gossip, where local farmers met on an evening to ridicule the ministry, tell fascinating stories or amuse passing tourists. That is, if anyone understood their thick Yorkshire dialect, which contained all the ingredients of a foreign language - including strange words and phrases. Some of the older locals spoke with an in depth knowledge of the area and its folk lore. Firmly believing the mysterious 'marsh fox' still thrived in the valley to the front of the farm. The farmers said the fox was larger than average, frightened of nothing and rarely seen. Whether this story be true or false, many lambs and fully grown sheep disappeared in the night, never to be seen again. They also told stories of how in the past the moors were an important place for religious rituals and sacrifice. Men and animals sacrificed to the bogs, the dark history of human sacrifice right here on these moors…

In the comfort of the saloon bar, stranger's quickly became friends, for there was nowhere better in England to enjoy the company of such warm friendly people as the Inns of North Yorkshire, above all, the Shepherd.

Of course, not all the local's were friendly. Some men lived high on the moors for reasons known only to them. For others, the ways of the moors became their undoing. You see, not everyone lived in the wilderness for scenery or solitude; some folk were short of knowing civilized. 'Wild men,' or so the locals said, whose land was best avoided.

Originally, Toby Jug Farm had served as a row of six cottages. Three cottages stood either side of a large central barn, just like two book stands. The farm house consisted of the three larger cottages, each with connecting interior doors, fine stone work and even finer oak beams which adorned the ceiling of every room and stood from floor to ceiling in some lower rooms. The stables, occupied the three smaller cottages, homes once occupied by weavers, containing strong double floors so as to support the weight of the looms, and proving eminently suitable for storing heavy loads of hay. Each loose box had once served as someone's living kitchen or sitting room, featuring high stone fireplaces and doorsteps. The stable windows, though now boarded up, retained the original stone mullions and the floors were paved in large stone flags.

At the end of the row, was an alleyway, which led into the old carriage room. Inside the carriage room was Geoff's blacksmiths shop and a room in which to store tack. This area had lots of space, plenty of height and two minute, church mullioned windows which looked out to the back of the farm, towards the graveyard and moors. We called this appendage, the tack room, storing saddles, bridles and fodder inside its splendid façade. At the back of the tack room was a small area where I loved to sit and listen to the sounds of the stables, or revise musical scores. Within this part, stood a glass fronted cabinet, used to store little used items, a small desk and a chair. My very own hide-away spot, where I could relax and read, wrapped warmly in horse blankets during the months of winter…

Ganador's loose box was the large living kitchen, next to the alleyway which looked out over the valley. His stable had dramatic views, all the way down to the gorge, a place where he could keep his eye on the other horses in the yard. A place we named Ganador's Kingdom.

\*

When I first saw Ganador, all of seven months ago, he was stabled and chained to the wall of a ramshackle cabin, in a scrap yard owned by Gypsies. His use, a guard horse to patrol the yard when the men were out.

There he stood, his enormous black eyes staring into mine, timeless eyes that melted me. Despite his angular appearance, I saw at a glance he was of the finest Spanish blood lines, his statuesque figure and Kingly arrogance shouted his superiority.

As he stood there, pretending to listen to distant murmurings, I gazed at a horse through the mists of time, a wild, fighting creature from centuries before.

And at that moment, I realized that no man would ever subdue Ganador, not fully, maybe not fractionally. This horse did not understand the whims of present day man, he did not understand fear and even less did he comprehend submission. Ganador was a horse from another time; line bred over centuries from the bravest lines of fighting horses, a horse to display prestige or carry a King-but sadly a horse born in the wrong century. During the seventeenth and eighteenth Centuries, the Iberian breed was the most sought after fighting horse in Europe...his name, The Battle Horse of King's. Horses like Ganador formed and shaped the course of Western civilization. Our world was born on his back, won through his bravery. He owes me nothing, whereas I owe him everything.

Almost seven months have passed since the arrival of Ganador, months filled with emotions ranging from the heights of elation to the deepest despair. After months of careful lunge work Ganador looks like a creature from the God's...the only missing item being his chariot. So many significant events have happened since the arrival of Ganador, that I often wonder why I should be so lucky to have found this King of creation. Possibly, the most dazzling event was Ganador's return to the Gypsy yard for Mark's Romany wedding. The Gypsy family begged me take Ganador back to the scrap yard to be the 'white holy horse.' You see, at a Romany wedding, the symbol of a white horse is a ritual as old as the hills, and some say more important than the vows or the ring. I could have said no to the Gypsies, but young Mark had been Ganador's friend, so I agreed and said yes...and memories of the wedding and Ganador's wish to please the boy refuse to go away. Part of me is still with the Gypsies and maybe always will be.

I cannot finish without saying 'thank you' to my Portuguese

friends, who enlightened me about the Iberian breed, told me that having a horse like Ganador is akin to owning a masterpiece, and I must never forget what he portrays. The same is true of the words of Fernando, my mentor, my learned professor. Fernando's words of great wisdom are related in this book, as a source of insight into the world and history of the Iberian Horse ... words of advice that if read with an open mind, give the satisfaction of discovering the truth.

Let me take you by the hand and lead you into Ganador's world, the world of a magnificent battle horse of centuries before. This book is the second part of his story; it's as much a story about his new life on the Yorkshire moors, as it is a story of the moorland people, who live within the enchanted area of Moonraker Heights...

*'The present is controlled and formed by the past'*

# *Summer* ... Yorkshire Moors
## ...1980

# 1. Moorland Magic

*Diary, Toby Jug Farm, August 14, 1980.*

'I can't forget the Romany wedding. Ever since Ganador returned to the Gypsy yard for young Mark's wedding my life has been trapped amongst the colors and customs of that other race ... the Gypsies. Why can't I return to the moor and be me?

At the strangest times I hear the same flamenco I listened to on Mark's wedding night, the same haunting melodies... the same rhythmic patterns. I must try to come down to earth and stop dreaming. The Gypsies have gone; maybe I'll never see them again....'

Last night, in my dreams, I returned to the Romany wedding. Under the glow of lanterns I watched my proud Spanish stallion dancing in a small cindered area. I heard flamenco artists shout and clap at the spectacle of 'el caballo blanco.' Then they began to play, creating rhythms, improvising melodies around Ganador's steps. A dancer entered the arena and walked over to Ganador. She looked very arrogant and wore a tightly fitted blood red dress that left nothing to the imagination. Her blue-black hair was threaded with rosebuds, the same rosebuds that were threaded through Ganador's mane. For a few moments she stood motionless, eyes half closed, absorbing the rhythm of horse and guitar. Suddenly, her body exploded with movement; wild, passionate flamenco baile. The dancer moved her hands sensually up and down her body, through her hair, and then high above her head. All the while she stamped in time with the stallions steps. Twirling to the left she held out her shawl and shouted 'Olé,' and to my astonishment Ganador twirled a pirouette ... he danced of his own free will! Striding backwards she held up the long frills of her dress whilst tapping out rapid footwork ... and Ganador advanced towards her in high passage, he was snorting with pleasure. Without touching the shawl he reared high into the air...

There were two guitarists playing now, their counter rhythms produced a dramatic effect. The sound was nothing less than orchestral. Unexpectedly, the flamenco stopped, leaving the exposed rhythm of martillo taps, mysterious and dark ... a sound that sends shivers down my spine.

When I awoke, I thought of Fernando's words. At the time, I hadn't understood his meaning...but now every syllable was crystal clear: 'Ancient legend describes the Iberian battle horse thus:

*'Long, long ago, before Spain and Portugal parted, the warriors of Southern Iberia taught their horses to dance. When the battles were none, the young horsemen relaxed to the music of the pipe and drum, and taught their combat horse to follow the movements of a dancer. Of course, the clever battle horses quickly learned to follow the steps of any dance, and to this day the prancing movements of the Spanish horse are referred to as dancing.'*

'What a lovely story ...So battle horses danced as well as fought on the battlefield?'

'If it pleased their master they danced, the young warriors taught their horses to dance, just for fun.'

'Do Spanish horses still dance?'

'To this day, the best Spanish horses dance,' and I thought of Ganador dancing and twirling at the Romany wedding, all of his own free will...

'Does this dance have a name?'

'When the best horses and best musicians come together as a spectator sport, it is called, 'the art of Andalucia.'

The following morning, I told Geoff about the flamenco melody living in my head. "It's interfering with my practice, like it's trying to take over my mind."

"Put a radio in every room, have a focal point to center on."

"Will it ever stop?"

"In time it will fade away. Made an impression on you hasn't it that Romany wedding? Must be your musical mind," he smiled and tweaked up my eyebrows. He thinks I am holding on to the music because deep down I don't want it to go. Maybe he's right. "Bet you don't hear it today though."

"Why not today?"

"We're shaking and rowing the hay, could be baling this afternoon. If I were you, I'd take Sue out shopping."

So I did just that. We drove down to Hebden the quickest way, straight to the end of the moorland road then down a perilously steep track shaded by broad leaf trees and pretty cottages. All the parking spaces were full, so I parked up on a narrow cobbled street behind the shops where children kicked footballs and washing lines stretched between high back to back terraces. On the old stone bridge we stopped, fed the ducks and gazed at the moors and hills. Hebden Bridge had to be the prettiest market town ever. On the main street trendy antique shops mingled with cafes, with not a supermarket in sight. A proper shopper's paradise!

"Can you imagine anyone calling Hebden a 'funky little town?'" Sue said suddenly. "It's an old fashioned market town, that's what it is." People make the place sound like Kensington market."

"I suppose you have to admit it is full of hippy types. All the shops are run by Londoners,' with a fascination for the word 'freedom.'"

I drove the second route back, the old stagecoach route that circled the fringes of Hardcastle Crags. Everything was perfect that day. Time passed slowly in summer, every second felt unhurried and relaxed. It gave me the sort of feeling I wanted to sink into ... closer to a dream than reality.

"Did you know nineteen eighty has been one of the warmest years on record?"

"As long as Geoff gets the hay in … the weather can do what it likes." And we returned home to a lazy day.

The afternoon of August the fourteenth was hot and sultry, probably one of the last golden days of summer. I stood close to the open window, listening to the sound of tractor's and voices suspended on the breeze … the sound of hay maker's everywhere, hard work but enjoyable. Already the perfume of new hay lingered in the air, on all the keys of the piano, inside every room. Powerful and sweet as honey, a heady scent of wild flowers, clover and lavender … a fragrance that took my senses by storm.

With a feeling of frustration, I placed my violin back in its case, tidied the music and closed the piano lid. Practice would have to wait … I'd much rather see the hay brought in. Out in the farmyard I leaned on the fence with Sue watching the old tractor chug slowly over the pasture.

"Look…" she pointed to an unknown place in the sky. "Blackbirds are flying away, without as much as a thank you." I watched them circle once over the meadow before taking wing across the valley.

"Song of summer flown away … I'll miss them." In summer, I opened all the mullioned windows wide so the blackbirds could join in with my practice, their sweet trills and wonderful cadenzas thrilled me … on a level so pure it just had to be the music of angels.

"Wonder where they're off to?"

"Someplace sheltered and warm…"

Thick billows of dust rose from the soil as the farm cart tilted first one way then the other on its way over the rutted track. Two helpers climbed down from the bales when the overloaded cart stopped near the footpath. Zachariah walked past the stables and up the track, back to his sheep farm on the moor. Willy cupped hands to mouth, he shouted: 'One hundred and ninety eight bales of good hay, sun bleached and golden … amazing for such a small meadow.' He waved, and turned down the path, to his cave house in the gorge.

"Chemistry lecturer turned hermit," I confided to Sue. "Wonder what tipped the balance?"

"Does it matter if he's happy?"

"Depends on what he's escaping from Sue..." And I went back to leaning on the fence, watching Ganador roaming free on his paddock, just him and the hills.

"I wish this moment could last forever." Time seemed to stand still in summer, every second felt unhurried and relaxed.

"Trouble is," replied Sue, "real life always returns."

"There's something so peaceful about watching a horse out in the open...something healing." I watched the stallion lift his head and stand motionless, all except for his eyes which followed the departing men. "He's tracking Zak and Willy until they're off the footpath...don't think Ganador will ever lose his guarding impulse." The stallion had the looks of a statue in the sunlight, his forehand shimmered in a haze of gold from the setting sun, and I felt overawed by his splendor.

"What's been going on?" asked Geoff as he climbed down from the hay cart. "Looked most odd from the bottom meadow," he smiled in a satisfied way and stretched out. "Put the kettle on Sue, three sugars for Carlton."

"Halifax Gazette wanted photos of Ganador..."

"Oh well, they must have no news."

"That's why I never read newspapers," said Carlton. "Filled with rubbish ... And that woman driving car wasn't local." He waited for my reply, as if already knowing the answer. "Where's she from?" he asked with a grimace.

"Leeds, she's editor of the Gazette."

"City dweller..." He spat to show his contempt. "That lots best kept at home, don't understand countryside." After unhitching the hay cart, Carlton took off his cap, looked me straight in the eyes, and said his piece. "Get thee up to Pub tonight Lass. That Lad o thine deserves a few beers. Nothing like beer for restoring lost energy tha knows." He turned the key, waited for the engine to splutter into life, and drove his ancient tractor rattling and steaming away up the farm track.

"That's Carlton's way of saying 'see you tonight.'"

"I'd not forgotten…"

On the evening of baling, Geoff took his helper's to the local Inn. Payment by food and drink was a ritual amongst hill farmers…money never changed hands, just help. Freely given and always returned.

Shortly after dusk fell, we strolled the short distance to the local Inn. There was a blazing sunset over the hills with flickering orange red lights that seemed to touch the summits with fire. Chairs and tables were placed outside on the cobbled area so as not to miss the moors answer to the northern lights. Tourists filled up most of the tables except for the ones where the farmers sat.

Carlton sat back in his chair and sighed, only then did he sip his beer. "Bloody lovely," he said. "First pint always tastes like nectar. I've been thinking about your oss. Money spinner if ever I saw one. Make tha sen some money Lad, sell photos to tourists. Tell em he's a breed brought oer in Spanish Armada. Believe owt they do."

"Where dost tha get ideas from?" Zachariah placed both elbows on the table, his medals flashed under the soft glow from a lantern. Polish by birth, Zachariah had eked out a living as a street musician in Warsaw. In nineteen forty three a group of German soldiers brought his meager career to an abrupt end when they shot him through the palms of both hands. Afterwards, he worked for the resistance, retiring to a small Yorkshire farm when his parents no longer needed him. The old soldier wore his medals on two days each week. On Sunday's, weather permitting he stood on the footpath outside his farm, waiting for any walker who might be interested in listening to his stories.

"Wish Elaine was still ere." Zak touched his cap and held a moment's silence "She always said there were nowt lovelier than a good oss." All the men touched their caps in respect.

"Let's drink t' memory of Elaine and sweetness of Geoff's hay." said Carlton. After placing his pint down, he gave Geoff a long look and said, "Did tha get stitched up good and proper when tha bought him?" Carlton had dared ask Geoff what everyone wanted to know.

"Swindled me out of three hundred quid-" Geoff still seethed over Adams little trick. There was a gasp of astonishment from the locals. "The Gypsy said I slapped his hand at the wrong time." Although Geoff had been repaid, he would never admit it to the locals. Some things were better overlooked.

"Tarred by same brush them Gypsies-" Carlton grimaced.

"What did you make of the Gypsies Norma?" asked the soft voice of Willy. The moors hermit sat where there was no light, the eyes of his rescued three legged fox glinted in the dark.

"When I took Ganador back to the scrap yard, I learned something important."

"I'm puzzled as to what a horse like him was doing with Gypsies," added Willy. He carried his pint over to the farmers table and sat next to Zak.

"I learned that being friends with a horse is more significant than fancy stables or buckets of oats."

"But he looked thin as a lath when you brought him up to moors," chipped in Carlton. "Tha can't feed an oss on nice words Lass."

"That I can't deny; its true he was kept as a Gypsy horse, fed straw and stabled in a dirty cabin. But the family gave him something else. They offered him friendship when nobody wanted him, and giving friendship to a rebel stallion is not in most men's rule book…"

"Why did nobody want him?" asked Willy.

"He'd become what's known as dangerous…and when a stallions termed 'dangerous' he quickly comes down the ladder of ownership."

"Tha can't get lower than a Gypsy yard," interrupted Carlton.

"What did the horse gain from being with Gypsies?" Willy spoke quietly, he was listening intently.

"Poor health and training as a guard horse," the farmers laughed at my honesty but, no-one spoke, so I went on. "The Gypsies respected Ganador with the same awe that some people save for a God."

"Why did they worship him?"

"Because Ganador is from the oldest Spanish blood lines, his forefathers were the bravest fighting horses in history...The battle horses of King's. Nowadays, only Gypsies and a few aficionados worship the old lines. No-one wants battle horses in today's world."

"He definitely looks like a battle Oss, but tha can never believe Gypsies Lass." Carlton leaned across the table to drain the last drops of Zak's beer, and quickly changed the subject. "If tha drinks this every night, thall never-ever need medicine..."

We left the Inn with its gathering of farmers just before eleven. Everything was perfect that night, exactly as it should be. The bales of hay were safely stacked in the barn; it was time to stop worrying about end of summer showers and damp misty mornings. The weather could do what it liked...now the hay was in.

"Can we listen to the quiet?" I asked slipping my arm through Geoff's. We stopped under the graveyards single lamp and listened.

The stillness of the moors had a sound all of its own, a silent pulse far beyond time and space, a sound that could only be heard if you concentrated hard. Sometimes, the stillness caused me to feel uncomfortable, even vulnerable.

"How can a never ending vibration come from total silence?" The answer to this fact always eluded me, always had.

"Something remains from everything that exists." replied Geoff...

"Who was it said nothing can come from nothing?"

"A very ancient Greek philosopher said that nothing changes and we must believe what we see."

"He'd certainly not visited the Yorkshire moors!" And we walked down the track laughing.

At the door, I felt an overwhelming sensation of the surrounding peace and quiet. Standing on tiptoe, I kissed Geoff on his cheek.

"What's that for?" he asked, seeming surprised.

"Because I'm happy" I felt tears come to my eyes, without reason or cause apart from emotion, and I thought of Mum's words...

'Always remember happiness is only a temporary condition.'

# 2. Dad's Birthday

*Toby Jug Farm, August 15.*

At nine a.m. precisely the phone rang. I knew the phone would ring for today was August the fifteenth…Dad's birthday.

"I'm not ringing at an inconvenient time am I?" Mum said worriedly. "I always forget about the time difference between England and Spain. Anyway … have you remembered the date?"

"How can I forget? Today's Dad's birthday, he'd be sixty three today." It was difficult sounding normal, keeping my voice relaxed and under control, for I knew that any hint of tension could upset her. There was an uncomfortable silence as Mum sighed and I covered the mouthpiece, breathing in deeply.

"Did you decide to include his name in El Pais?"

"What would be the point…I know I've done everything wrong, but does it really matter?"

"Dad's gone, how can it matter?"

"Well I'll tell you my next piece of news." Mum changed the subject pronto. There was never any time to lose and sometimes I couldn't keep up with her thoughts. She said I failed to move on quick enough.

"I joined the flamenco appreciation group last week, and guess who I met at the first meeting?"

"Who did you meet?"

"Does the name Pepe mean anything to you?"

"Pepe from the Romany wedding…"

"Well, Pepe came along as guest artist, and in the interval I told him all about you and Ganador. He looked amazed when I said the name Ganador! And then, he told me all about the Romany wedding, and how you had taken the stallion back down to the Gypsy yard for Mark and Evita's wedding.

Pepe explained all about rites and customs with the Romany people. 'A white holy horse; is a ritual as old as the hills...as important as the vows and the ring'. And I believed his every word. Anyhow, to cut a long story short, he invited me out! He said he'd love to show me his Seville, take me to some of the places where he drove the carriage with Ganador.

I do wish you'd been there when Pepe told me the stories of Ganador's exploits, he really was naughty! Ganador could open stable doors, unfasten ropes...and you'll never believe this...the horse knew how to count up to ten by striking the ground with his hoof! He said he'd never forget the day when Ganador decided to visit the mansion, all by himself...

'The Master and me were enjoying coffee in the breakfast room when I heard someone knocking on the door. I walked over to the window to see who it was...and there stood Ganador banging on the knocker with his nose. The moment he spotted me at the window he came over and looked into the room, his big black eyes pressed against the glass. When he saw the master, he began whinnying to get his attention. I swear the stallion put on a show that morning, as if to say, 'look at me - look at my splendor.' We stood there gazing out through the French windows, watching Ganador perform the airs of piaffe, passage and levade, right there on the breakfast terrace. He was incredible...Mama Mia! The master ordered a maid take out a breakfast tray, and what we witnessed amazed us for a second time. Ganador sipped from the cup, and then ate the two rolls, just like a gentleman, hardly leaving a crumb. We were dumbfounded.

'A creature of more than animal intelligence,' Antonio declared. The master appeared most impressed by Ganador's reasoning powers, though later that day he walked up to the stable yard and terminated the employment of the two grooms on duty that morning.'"

"Whatever for…?"

"For failing to notice Ganador had escaped from his stable and gone down to the house. Pepe said the Master was a hard man and his decisions were final."

"What did you make of Pepe?"

"He's very polite, exceedingly rich and owns three flamenco bars!"

"But why does he work for the Master?"

"It's not about money, more about history. The Master owns a Yeguada with some of the purest Carthusian blood lines in Spain. According to Pepe, horses like Ganador changed the course of history. He said our civilization was born on their backs, won through their bravery. He even told me a bit of their history:

'Long, long ago', he said 'The warriors of southern Iberia bred the bravest and most beautiful battle horse in the world. These noble creatures were called the Battle Horse of King's and were fearless and incredibly proud. Willing to take their master's to the ends of the earth, prepared to give of their lives'. The Battle horse of King's was a force wanted by every country. He also told me that Ganador's forefathers were bred to fight, and I must never confuse his bravery with temper. Pepe's passionate about this breed of horse, and it could be, because they are very nearly extinct. He also told me the Master ought never to have sent Ganador away for breaking, because they didn't understand him … and how selling him to England, lost Spain one of its oldest bloodlines. The way he told me the story of Ganador touched my heart, and I believed his every word."

"Maybe you fell in love with his words Mum? It's so easy to do. But you must have formed an opinion about Pepe, the man…"

"He's a charming romantic with a hidden agenda. That's who Pepe is."

On placing the receiver down I felt relief, for I didn't want to be happy. Unlike Mum's world … I'd not moved on. I still woke up thinking of Dad. Was this how grief worked? Was it a gradual healing process when hurting became less- A time when happy days were allowed to return, mixed in with sad ones- And after that, what happened to the memory? Was the memory forgotten … lost forever?

After talking with Mum, I looked in my diary…across from August fifteenth I'd written: 'Ring Dad…63 today!' At that instant, the door slammed and Geoff walked in. Quickly I closed the diary, but not before he'd seen the tears.

"Shoeing nails, I always forget them." Geoff's blacksmiths nails were kept in the kitchen so as not to become rusty. "Wish you'd stop looking at diaries, it's not normal. Think of the future and stop dwelling on the past…try to be positive."

"Today was Dad's birthday, but now there's no Dad to see, no Dad to hear. But I can dream about him, or are dreams not positive enough?"

"Better let you get on with it then." As Geoff went out, he closed the door softly, without its usual bang. So I got on with it, and had a good cry. Afterwards, I slowly and painfully crossed the words out… Memories came flooding back of Dad's birthday last year, I remembered every moment.

I'd flown out to Seville for his sixty second birthday. He waited outside arrivals; he always stood in the same spot, so I wouldn't miss him. Once in the car I asked him why he worked such long hours, but he didn't listen, he laughed.

"There's nothing wrong with work love… I don't want retirement thrust upon me, at least not yet."

"But you are getting older Dad."

"You should never argue on a birthday…let's not talk about work." So I sat back and listened, time spent with him was much too precious to waste. "As a special treat, I bought tickets for a Doma Vaquera display, its tomorrow evening at eight."

"Is the display near Seville?"

"Somewhere near Jerez at a bull breeding ranch-and Jose the barber tells me it's not to be missed."

"You spoil me Dad."

"But I enjoy spoiling you."

"Have you seen much Doma Vaquera riding Dad?"

"A little ... and I've become quite addicted. It's a style of cowboy training that allows the rider to carry out his daily work with fighting bulls in the fields without being injured ... an honored Spanish equestrian tradition!"

At six p.m. the following day, we headed towards Jerez de la fronterra, an area where bull breeding, sleek caballos and sherry barons abound. We passed through a landscape entirely dedicated to agriculture, where mile after mile of precision planted crops grew side by side, amid meticulous shimmering grassland, with not a blade out of place.

"This is what's called 'robot farming,' it needs one man, lots of machines, and irrigation sprinklers the length of a swimming pool."

"Certainly not a walker's paradise is it?"

"But this is how the money is made."

Just before seven we arrived at our destination, a splendid Cortijo, standing at the top of a long palm lined driveway. The Cortijo had the looks of a palace; its high singular dome dominated the surrounding land. The terrain stretched out for hundreds of hectares, until disappearing into woodlands of cork oak and pine. After walking under a high arch, we arrived in the internal courtyard, where the families' carriages were parked. Past the courtyard stood the equestrian facilities ... I had never seen such luxury. The three blocks of internal stables were set in a walled compound, of Moorish design; and in the center of each Cuadra stood a fountain. Olympic sized training areas lay positioned behind the stables, and to the right a private bull ring with seating. On the left stood the indoor school, Arabic in design and completely lined with mirrors.

Nothing seemed real that night. Everything loomed larger than life; the spectators in their colorful sombreros, the shining horses, a Mexican band playing Gershwin's summertime ... Dad's favorite melody. It was all too good to be true.

"Doma Vaquera is much more than any obsession. It's a way of life..." Dad had to shout to be heard. The spectators never stopped talking, laughing or shouting comments to friends across the way.

They'd come out to enjoy the evening and the atmosphere could not have been happier.

The first displays were of pure Doma Vaquera, showing exercises needed when working cattle in the fields. Immediate starts, turns, sliding stops and side steps, every movement packed with energy and quick as lightning.

"Only a horse with strong joints, perfect balance and flexibility could use its hind legs at such speed and stay sound. There's no place for the average horse in this sport..." I was really talking to Dad, but must have been overheard.

"The very best working horses are old line Spanish or American saddle stock, but most are Hispano-Arab because of their speed and stamina. Is this the first time for you guys?" asked a woman in a red sombrero with a slow Texan drawl. "And yes, only the best horses can carry out the movements."

During the interval, a long bar opened in the bull ring, serving the Andalucian snack of Serrano ham and goat's cheese with chunks of warm garlic bread.

"Why does food taste better when eaten out under the stars?"

"Being happy with your surroundings is more important than a well set dinner table!" replied Dad as he tucked into a second helping.

On returning to our seats I heard the sound of two instruments, a Spanish guitar and a violin. The violin was held like a cello, its body resting on the man's knee. A glorious reverberation of an Eastern melody silenced everyone. The men played the opening bars of a Tarantas, over and over again, faster and faster, until the spectators shouted approval. Perhaps it was the sherry wine, or the music of that single guitar, perhaps the sleek horses played a part. Who knows? I only know it happened then, at that moment, that I recognized all I needed to know about Doma Vaquera and its followers ... without a question being asked. When the lights went down, a quiet admiration settled over that noisy, laughing, audience. Now, the shouting turned to whispering, the audience waiting for the next rider in what could only be described as awe.

To the haunting sounds of the string duo, before a hushed

audience, a lone horseman entered the arena. He held his reins in his left hand, in his right hand he carried a thirteen foot bamboo pole...called a 'garrocha' used for moving fighting bulls in the fields. Sliding to a halt he deftly removed his sombrero, held it across his chest and bowed. He had such powerful charisma; his eyes looked so tragically noble, and my heart went out to him. Did nothing matter now, except to maintain this pride, this spirit of the past? Maybe his pride was too inbred to be discarded? Had the rider been born in the wrong century, just like his horse?

The horse pranced into canter, dancing through figures of eight, circles and side steps, all the while his garrocha traced outlines of his movements in the sand, correct in line and contour.

"His tracings look like crop circles, they couldn't be more perfect." Mum sounded thrilled. "How is it possible to ride with such skill, whilst simultaneously drawing figures in the sand with a pole?"

"And remember he's holding the reins in one hand..."

Thrusting the point of the pole into the center of a circle, the horse twirled like a ballerina...and during every turn the rider's body bent lower under the pole, his sombrero never moving, never touching the pole. Now, the horse went into rein back, there was nothing held back, horse and man giving of their all. The rider placed the point of the garrocha in the center of the arena, and with the horse moving rapidly backwards traced some imaginary figure in the sand. Sliding to a halt he stood back from his tracing, and then he bowed and held out his hand. There before me was a faultlessly traced heart shape ... in its center, his initials M.M.

The display came to an end in the usual way, with a fiery gallop round the arena, the rider leaning forwards, his garrocha carried high, as if charging at some imaginary enemy. To the music of a single guitar, the horse slid to a halt, reared high into the air and bowed on one knee...the display at an end.

"You guys haven't seen anything yet," said the woman in the red sombrero. "He rides his second horse without holding the reins." And so he did, he entered in high passage riding a silver grey stallion...there were no reins in his hands. The rider's hands were placed on his hips ... and then I noticed the reins, which were discreetly clipped to his belt. The man and horse were in a league all of their very own.

Within the display I'd felt a magic, a respect for what is purely Andalucian, an immense pride in showing to their audience the honored equestrian tradition of Doma Vaquera, a type of training which exists in every country in the world ... though Spanish in origin.

"I wonder where you get your love of horses from..."

"I don't know Dad, but whenever I'm with them, I leave all my worries behind."

At that moment the grandfather clock in the sitting room noisily chimed eleven. Time to leave memories behind and carry on with today, just like Mum had. Placing the diary back in the desk drawer I opened the secret drawer where I'd hidden the program of that night at the Cortijo, concealed, out of sight. I hadn't felt ready to relive its memories, not until now...

## La Doma Vaquera y los Garrochistas

*'La Doma Vaquera and the art of the Garrochistas are two of the most traditional equestrian disciplines in Spain, and the world. These equestrian traditions promote and preserve this speciality for its time-honored importance, making it possible for an ever increasing number of enthusiasts to follow the arts. Related to the work performed on the fields with cattle, and before that the movements performed on the battlefield.'*

As I read the program I felt a warm glow, the kind you feel when sitting in front of a glowing fire on a freezing cold night, and I remembered listening to the end of one of Dad's stories: 'And the Spanish fighting horse became the horse of courtly splendor, famed, sought after, unrivalled. And a new art form grew which took Europe by storm, when the natural abilities of the Spanish horse moved from the battlefield to the ménage...'

# 3. The Affiliation

On arriving home, Geoff and Sue had just finished unloading a classy thoroughbred.

"Two hours to get her loaded, and as long again to persuade her to come out. She's terrified of the ramp." Geoff looked exhausted.

Here we go again I thought, almost the month of September, the beginning of problem horse season. This was the time when horses refused by large yards ended up with us for one last attempt. I thought of the most recent, a beautiful chestnut stallion that had learned to throw his rider into orbit, or even worse into the path of a car, all without a moment's hesitation.

We found the cause when Sue clipped him. The horse had extensive spur damage, with skin that was sore and angry looking, painful to the touch of a finger never mind a heel or sharp spur. I remembered how we padded the inside of the girth with foam before covering it with sheepskin and wore soft trainers when riding him, not the usual boots. How we spent hours gaining his trust. I remembered the day I rode him in front of his owner, by then he'd learned to trust me and was obeying my every wish.

"Would you like to ride him?" I'd asked. "He doesn't need spurs any longer; he's very sensitive to the leg." The woman's white face and clenched fists said it all. She never rode him again. Before she took him away, I said the words I'd heard Fernando saying many times:

'Always keep in mind that when everything fails, rebellion remains.' The horse was sold at auction the following week ... a meat man bought him. I felt sad and angry. Owners always took their unspoiled horses to large classy yards- this was a fact of life. Less expensive yards like ours existed for tragedies. Geoff thought we should call the yard 'last chance saloon.' I said never…

The phone rang just as we sat down to dinner. Geoff went to answer, "I'll put her on." he said. "Do her good to think about something else…" and he handed me the phone. It was Val's unmistakable voice, she always sounded bright and breezy, made me feel half asleep.

"A plea from the heart, I need help and fast!"

"Spill the beans Val."

"Recently, I've been thinking about the merits of affiliating the local riding club to the British Horse Society, all that advice on insurance, better prestige and so on. Let the good old B.H.S. lend a hand."

"Sounds like a good idea…"

"However, there's a snag, the affiliation people need to see two class lessons plus a lecture demo. So, I've rung for your help…I thought if we worked together…" Val had a way of melting people. No matter how hard you tried, it was impossible not to fall under her spell. Val was an organizer, and a good one. Perhaps it was due to her Rodean education and mixing with important people. Her latest little job was to organize an M.P. - I sometimes felt that Val could organize the world. She'd been there and done it as Geoff put it, and in a way I suppose he was right.

"This bunch, know zero about the finer points of riding, all they think about is muck spreading and sheep shearing. So, my plan is to collect say twelve riders for next Saturday, and line them up at my place- ready for me and you to knock them into shape, prior to B.H.S. day. Please Norma…"

"I can try. When's the Day of Judgment?" I heard a huge sigh of relief…

"You're a star! And we have three full weeks."

"How about dropping the number to six riders, far more manageable than twelve?"

"Yes I know, but half of them never turn up... so if I invite twelve..." Three years ago Val decided to form a local riding club, which quickly became known as the 'Moor and Vale.' She organized the odd hunter trial, summer outings, Christmas dinner and so on. It was all light hearted fun, but the club kept riders in touch, and the membership was growing steadily.

As I put the phone down I became aware of Geoff and Sue listening to my every word. Geoff said it would do me good to get out, and Sue offered to skip her weekend breaks, and so, I became involved in affiliating our local riding club.

The planned lesson was a nightmare, not even simple terms were understood. I could have been speaking another language.

"What do you expect from the offspring of hill farmers? These people don't spend evenings reading dressage manuals, they prefer filling subsidy forms in." Val hissed from her summer house, located behind letter C. "I told you they're hopeless."

And as for turning left or right, well that was chaos, so I did the only thing possible, I ordered the riders to dismount and take the horses out of the arena, before continuing the lesson on foot.

"Next Saturday," I shouted. "I expect to see better work. You have one full week, or seven full days, to practice changing the rein in walk, preferably on your horse."

"I should have organized training days, but no-one seemed interested... they all wanted hunter trials."

"Why cross bridges before we come to them? There's always next week, or a miracle."

"So paddling through streams and jumping twigs mean absolutely nothing?"

"Not if there's insufficient flat work."

On the second Saturday, there was a definite improvement, the strict discipline and sergeant major style shouting had started to pay dividends. In only one week, my riders could walk and trot in line, change the rein and show a transition. I was amazed, until Val let the cat out of the bag.

"Did you know," she said miserably "I visited every farm last week, and marched them through turning left and right? Get off your backsides and get on with it." I told them "Or you won't have a riding club."

"And I thought it was my shouting."

"What do you think … is there a chance?"

"I think; we have a definite chance if the leader turns up, as he's the only one who knows left from right." Tim, the leader of my rider's, acted as headmaster of the local school, the one at the bottom of the Steep's. I couldn't do without him.

"Don't worry … he'll turn up. I'm collecting him in the horse box"

The affiliation lesson was held on a windswept field, close to the town of Huddersfield. There were two marked out schooling areas, one for working in, and the other for the lesson. Val stood with Caroline from the British Horse Society, who carried a board and seemed to never stop writing.

Two horses bolted and jumped the barrier, a third refused to move, but the remaining eight put on a decent show. I remember feeling quite proud of them. But by far, the biggest miracle was the fact that nobody fell off. Val told the representative that it was everyone's first taste of instruction, and I heard Caroline say, she was most surprised. So Val invited her for lunch in the local pub, where we plied her with drinks.

"What topic is the lecture on?" Caroline asked me at the bar.

"Bits and bitting," I replied "there are so many confusing combinations, that I think it wise to spell out the dangers of certain types of mouth pieces immediately"

"Always a good choice." she said happily, so I handed her yet another sherry. The lecture was held in a small room smelling of beer, which joined on to the saloon bar. In the room were some desks, and on every one, there laid a striking copy of our bit's and bitting lecture notes. At the top of each were the words, 'Moor and Vale Riding Club, West Yorkshire, B.H.S. affiliated' and at the bottom, 'England's Heartland of Equitation.' Both were in startlingly bold type. The thought did cross my mind, that we had not yet received that honor, at least not yet.

After Caroline departed, we agreed the day had been a great

success. All we had to do now was organize a display.

"What are we doing for the demonstration? Because we'll have to toe B.H.S. lines you know."

"Lungeing and long reining – I love the sound of the words. I wonder how Geoff might feel about bringing Ganador along. Just for show of course, with Fred and Donovan as demo horses."

"Does he know?"

"I'm ringing him tonight."

"Ganador only has two paces as yet."

"You mean he can't canter?"

"Has no idea about the pace, whether his hang up is mental or physical is unknown…" But whatever I said, didn't put Val off, if anything she seemed keener.

"Who wants canter? Just let him enjoy himself in front of spectators. No doubt Caroline and the Yorkshire farming community will love him whatever he does. I'm billing him as special guest star."

Later that evening, Geoff answered the phone. I heard him say "Don't be silly Val." His voice had the sound of a growl, a warning one. "Correct work from the ground in front of spectators and B.H.S. officials could prove to be damn tricky." And Geoff went silent, he had to, he couldn't get a word in. I was sure I heard Val's bubbly voice from the other side of the room. "Has Norma put you up to this? Well, just remember it's not a rodeo." were his final words.

"What did Val say?"

"She wants me to do a display on work from the ground."

"But who are you displaying?"

"Fred for lunging techniques, and Donovan in long reins-"

"Val's very persuasive … I must ask her how she does it. Have you also agreed to display Ganador?"

"Well yes," the tone of his voice had lost its previous authority - he sounded sheepish "But only for show."

\*

29

Meanwhile, Val was hard at work, printing up large glossy posters, on which Geoff was depicted as a ring master, together with long whip and top hat. The horses appeared to be jumping through hoops, all but for Ganador, and he looked rather like a unicorn ... a flying unicorn complete with wings.

"Everyone wants to see Ganador, he's star material Norma. You can't keep him under wraps forever." Val cheerfully pinned a second poster on the doors of Hebden Bridge tourist office. "Only two more, Todmorden and Mytholmroyd, and then everyone can come along."

"But people will think it's a circus Val."

"Anything goes in advertising, you should know that. Ganador will draw the crowds in."

As usual Val was correct, for on the evening of the display, the indoor school of Equus Riding Academy Huddersfield was full to capacity- even the B.H.S. officials had to sit at the back.

"It may be at the back ... but it's a table with a difference, we have to make visitors welcome, so I've given them a bottle of wine and a tray of canopies, which I made myself."

"I wondered why they were at the back."

The display opened with Ganador. Geoff entered the school with the stallion on the short rein, in Spanish Walk, a movement he had only recently learned, but taken to like a duck to water. I stood at the bottom of the gallery steps with the microphone, answering questions about the horse, type of movement, and training technique.

"Sorry Norma," said Val. "Can you hand me the mike? I've forgotten to introduce Geoff ... I need to say a few words."

"First of all Ladies and Gentlemen a special thank you to Geoff!" Ganador halted on the center line and displayed a perfect piaffe, he was enjoying himself immensely. "Tonight we have a unique guest, Yorkshire's very own Ganador V – a horse with star quality, from the Royal Sevilla Stud." As the applause grew louder Ganador's piaffe became higher, my heart raced faster than I thought possible. When Val handed the mike back, she said, "I told you he'd bring the house down, what an incredible horse, tell the audience there will be time for photographs at the end of the show."

Sue, Ganadors groom had turned the stallion out perfectly, he looked gorgeous, so I gave her a 'special thank you' over the microphone, and again the audience applauded - until she finally stood up and waved.

Geoff led Ganador around the school in Spanish Walk on every third stride. The music was Rumba Flamenco which blasted out over loudspeakers, and surprisingly but very definitely, Ganador's steps gave the appearance of following the rhythm. He was dancing, and enjoying every moment. The spectators began to join in the fun, even the officials were clapping … Val was dancing.

When the music stopped Sue took Ganador from Geoff, and handed over Fred. He behaved perfectly, displaying work on the lunge and some of the techniques used in lunging faultlessly, I felt so proud.

"Only mention the equipment allowed by the B.H.S." whispered Val. She pushed a note into my hand, which read, 'snaffle bit and side reins only!'

Following Fred's display, Geoff worked Donovan in long reins to the music of Strauss, and once again I felt blissfully happy watching such perfect understanding between man and horse. At this point the spectators wanted to hear from the man himself, and Val took the mike over to Geoff. Before she gave it to him she made an announcement "Geoff will see any problem horses now …" and the first problem horse was led in, it belonged to the school,

"She refuses to lunge to the right…" the assistant said "Swerves back left immediately." And so she did, each time the direction changed to the right, the mare spun to the left.

"I'll have to go back to the box" Geoff whispered in my ear "For the longer whip … Lead her round the school, halt then walk, and hold the whip backwards aiming for impulsion into walk."

The spectators waited for the moment of truth - I knew there wouldn't be one.

"Begin at the beginning…" he said, "by teaching the horse to lead. This is where communication begins, the halter, rope and whip." When Geoff took over the lungeing, I could have heard a pin drop. He didn't need a mike, no one spoke or moved.

"The trainer must follow the horses shoulder, framing the horse between hand and whip is rule one, rule two is that the whip must be long enough to touch the horse." And the mare lunged perfectly, on both left and right reins.

"Tell Geoff to throw a schooling fee in Norma, I would." Caroline said stepping down from the balcony. "Just imagine not knowing how to lunge correctly … and a B.H.S. approved school too."

Mum rang up later that night, "Well … Did you pass. Is the club B.H.S. recognized?"

"Yes, we passed! The horses behaved perfectly, and everyone enjoyed the show"

"How could anything possibly go wrong when Val organized it, the girl's a marvel …Just one other thing, are you keeping your spirits up?"

"When I don't have time to think, it's a resounding yes."

"Well you know how to deal with it then." she said "There's always a way…"

*

At eleven a.m. on the morning following the show, Val rapped on the window pane.

"Are you in?" she mouthed on the glass. I opened the window "Fancy a trip out?" I knew the trip was something to do with the riding club "Thought I'd take you up to Eagles Nest, it's almost time to hold our first 'affiliated' hunter trial. I think the place will be ideal."

So I grabbed wellingtons and rain proofs, before obediently following her into the yard.

"Quick!" she said "I've left the engine running … I jammed a brick on the accelerator. Damn thing has a nasty habit of dying on me" Val's vintage land rover was shaking and rattling behind the stables, "You won't need wellies where we are going. It's not moorland like this-" She pointed to the surrounding land, which included mine.

"I'm taking you to the top of a mountain. Somewhere magical, where there's no mud. Hikers boots are more appropriate"

After passing through Hebden Bridge, we crossed to the opposite side of the river Calder, where a winding track took us up into the clouds.

"We can't drive any higher. No road surface. A real car wrecker" Val drummed her fingers on the dashboard and gazed at a passing cloud "Lovely view of Stoodley Pike isn't it?"

"The views are incredible. But how do we get to this Eagles Nest? Don't say I have to walk. Not up a cliff face" It's no wonder Val's wearing hiking boots. The second half of the track consisted of deep holes, rocks and loose stones. All the soil had washed away.

"If you look up you can just see it." 'Eagles Nest,' stood perched on what must be one of the highest points in North West Yorkshire. It was built like a medieval castle, had an amazing view of Stoodley Pike and looked down on the towns in the valley.

"But where will the horseboxes park?"

"Right here of course. And then the competitors can proceed on hoof or foot. It's entirely up to them. Any cross country enthusiast will marvel at this setting. Just love it."

"I do hope your right."

"I would have preferred somewhere lower, but Caroline's kind offer made it difficult to say no. Can you imagine, living up here, on your own?"

"You mean Caroline the BHS woman?" And Val just nodded. When I heard the name Caroline, I felt a wave of shock. I'd never imagined that Caroline lived even higher than me. She looked more like a semi detached dweller, one of those proper people. She definitely didn't give the impression of being a mountain top loner.

After a hike of some fifteen minutes or so, we arrived at our location, a seventeenth century farmhouse enclosed by high walls.

"Probably the walls protect the farm from blizzards. Keep the snow from the door."

"I would imagine there's no shortage of blizzards up here, it's almost sixteen hundred feet high!"

"It must be tough living up here in winter, even tougher than the moors, if that's possible." But I had to admit the views were stunning. Maybe, they were even more incredible than my own.

All round me were the distant outlines of hills, and glints of rock, except to the south where there was nothing but clouds and the odd hazy glimpse of a mill chimney in the valley. The farm land on the mountain top was flat and well drained. Fifteen acres of perfection ... Caroline's farm had everything, except parking.

"Not a trace of mud." Val said blissfully "And look at the obstacles ... They are a natural part of the field." And so they were. There was a stream, a ditch and tree trunk on its side, all easy to negotiate, followed by two duck ponds, one at either side of the farm. Sorting out time came two canter strides after the second duck pond, in the form of a low stone wall which was situated on the edge of the flat land. My stomach turned when I looked over the wall.

"But I can only see clouds..." The farm land fell steeply away; there was no landing area to be seen. "It's a lot to ask of a horse."

"Unlike their riders, horses are not stupid. Horses can sense the unseen. I thought of calling it 'parachute' jump."

At that exact moment Caroline rode out of the stable yard. She was mounted on a jet black thoroughbred, a horse stamped all over with quality, that inimitable look of class.

"Was she very expensive Caroline?" I asked "She's classy." It was clear the mare had the finest breeding lines. No doubt a horse bred from champions, for one purpose only, to win races.

"She's what's called a slow racehorse. Nobody else bid but me!" Caroline leaned forwards, her voice low. Her eyes twinkled and she smiled ever so demurely. "But listen to this ... I had a visitor last night." Val seemed interested. She's holding the reins now so Caroline can dismount "A handsome s.a.s. man! He knocked on the kitchen door just before eleven, said he was on 'mission survival,' and could he sleep in the barn?"

"But how do you know he's s.a.s.?" asked Val, drawing even closer.

"Because the word 'Army' is written all over his face Val. He wanted me to ring his commanding officer and check him out, but I believed him. So I made him sandwiches with a pot of tea. Have a break in your survival mission I said."

"But he could be a mass murderer."

"Don't be silly Val. What would a mass murderer be doing up here? There's no one to murder, except me."

"Is he still here?" Val hissed.

"Yes..." Caroline hissed back "He's enjoying his breakfast in the barn ..."

The time was just before two when Val's land rover rattled into the stable yard.

"Is Geoff giving a course on stable management ... to the police?" she asked "Because, I can see two police cars parked in the stable yard."

"I wonder what's going on ..."

"Must be something grim-" Val always knew about important matters. "They only send two cars out when it's serious. I'm glad I live where it's safe." Her tone was conversational, but I knew she meant every word. As if to bear out Val's theory, armed police were spread out across the yard, "There's one taking up position on the footpath ... How bizarre."

"We have reason to believe a wanted man is heading for the moors. It's possible he's on the Yorkshire side of the Penine Way." The officer went on with his advice, "It would be wise to collect all dangerous items together, hide them away and lock them up."

"What's a dangerous item?" questioned Val. The officer smiled and started to explain the endless possibilities to be found within the words.

"Anything sharp, knives, nails, hammers, or such like. If I lived up here I'd take the cutlery to bed-" By the time the officer had finished his warning, my hands were sweating with fear. Something they never do.

"I won't be sleeping tonight." said Sue "Unless it's with the dogs. I know we are out in the wilds, but there are always strange goings-on, at least there are up here. The place seems to attract weird events. You have to admit it Norma."

"Where's Geoff anyway?" I asked, wondering why he chose the most awkward times to be away.

"He's driven over to Halifax tractor hunting I do believe."

Undismayed, the police officer papered the dining room table with artist's impressions of his wanted man, long haired, short haired, bearded and clean shaven.

"What's he wearing?" said Val "Can you tell me?"

"Army combat suit I believe. Tells everyone he's an s.a.s. officer"

Val dug me in the ribs. "Is there anything else we need to know?" She was thinking along the same lines. There was a definite similarity to Caroline's visitor, but no more than that.

"I think I've got the picture officer." I said "You have made everything clear" Val escorted the policeman back to his car, and within seconds I'd rung Caroline.

"Caroline … the police are at my farm. They're searching for a dangerous man, who's claiming to be an S.A.S. officer."

"I still have the telephone number he gave me. I'll ring you back after I've checked him out." And within minutes she replied. "Yes he is s.a.s. - what a relief! The person who replied said the Yorkshire moors have everything men need to become familiar with solitude and wild terrain…"

We held the hunter trial in the first week of September, thinking we may possibly beat the weather. But the day was not what we had planned. Although it dawned sunny but cold, a sudden gale blew the fence numbers down, and heavy rain stopped all but the most ardent cross country riders from taking part. But that said, there were still eighteen entries.

Geoff brought Ganador up, a miracle on such a day seeing how he hated riding in the rain. Although, he only walked or trotted round, 'just for fun,' he still came in second. The winning horse and Ganador were the only entries to jump off the edge of Caroline's field then disappear into clouds, without a refusal.

"I'd be ashamed to bring that skeleton out," remarked Caroline as she looked at the winning horse. "Thin as a lath, galloped round in torrential rain and then left to stand in the rain."

"What some people will do to win a rosette" added Geoff from the warmth of the barn.

"Exactly-" replied Val; and when Val said 'exactly' in that tone of voice, the conversation was at an end

Caroline served bacon wraps through the kitchen window- Val made coffee in paper cups, whilst I timed the entries. The families of the hardy eighteen sat on bales of hay in the barn … keeping Caroline and Val busy all morning. Following the hunter trial I walked to the end of the perfect pasture and gazed at the surrounding wilderness. No horizon could be seen … just low cloud stretching into a sea of hilltops and the faintest howling of a wind somewhere in the distance. All around me, the moist peat earth steamed garlands of chiffon mist into the air, the last of summer's warmth just floating away. Winter was on its way.

# 4. Run with the Stars

*Diary, September 24, Harvest Moon...*

'After the hunter trial, the calendar appears to be going backwards. Suddenly, the weather is returning to summer, days are warm, cloudless and still. Geoff tells me its due to warm air from the Gulf Stream, and it's called, Indian summer. I don't care what it is...I love every minute! This morning from the bedroom window I saw a fox! His color was shimmering red with a white star and chest. I watched him make his way down the footpath and over the stile, never have I seen such perfectly balanced movement, he seemed to flow along the ground. At a guess I'd say his tail looked as long as his body, maybe even longer. It's my first sighting of a wild fox, and I will never forget his image...

Today is orchestra rehearsal. It's the first get together after summer, which means a drive to Manchester and back. How I hate leaving the farm on such a lovely day...'

Geoff was already riding Ganador when I peeped through the school door. He walked him round the school on a long rein, repeating the silent communication between man and horse that starts with riding straight lines. Only when this became established would he teach him the aids to change direction, or turn left or right. In the silvery light of early morning Ganador looked unreal. His aura of nobility felt overpowering. How I loved these special moments before the day began, they were times I treasured, magical times.

"What brings Norma out at such an early hour?"

"Geoff! I've seen a fox."

"What was he doing?"

"He flowed along the footpath and over the stile then disappeared towards the gorge."

"Maybe he's looking for Willy."

"Hope he's not injured." Any fox in need of help instinctively headed towards Willy's cave house. "Changing the subject, have you remembered today's orchestra rehearsal?"

"How can I forget? You've written it all over the calendar so I can't see the dates."

"Might be a long day"

"Are the brass section propping the bar up again?" Geoff laughed, knowing full well that brass players always propped bars up. "Must be all that blowing they do."

So I sat in the gallery and gazed at Ganador in a pool of silvery light enjoying five minutes of heaven... until Geoff reminded me of the date.

"Have you remembered tonight?" he asked. "It's harvest moon."

"How could I ever forget?" Geoff had taken me to the highest point of the moors on the night of last year's harvest moon. 'Right place at the right time is half the battle won,' he'd said. It was the first time I'd seen a harvest moon or followed moon phases, but I never would forget the thrill of being there and gazing at the heavens in all their majesty, of looking up at the stars, and feeling mesmerized by the mystery of life and the splendor of everything around me.

"Just hope I'm back in time..."

As I walked back to the house, I remembered last night and the phone call. We were in the dining room starting to eat when the phone rang.

"Let it ring." I said "dinner will be cold."

"Might be important." replied Geoff already heading for the sitting room. Then I heard his voice, his tone had a pay attention quality that made me want to listen, so I sat very still and eaves dropped.

"It's a dodge he's learned, lying down when ridden avoids work.

Either the rider's not firm enough or there's a remote possibility of pain." he paused - I thought I heard a note of disgust in his voice. "You can't starve an animal into submission." Again he went quiet. "Well I wouldn't know where the pain is, not without seeing the horse. It's a black and white world compared to ours…"

When he returned to the table I said "Why do you waste time and effort lecturing owners? No-one listens. They get rid of difficult horses and buy another."

"That is entirely up to them, so long as they understand there's no such thing as a problem horse."

"We own a problem horse. He can fly though the air or dance on the spot, and his Spanish walk is amazing, but moving forwards like a normal horse seems beyond him. I should have left him at the scrap yard with the Gypsies…"

"Life would have been easier and safer." Geoff pulled his face, the way he did when he wanted to make me laugh "But until his hind quarters and back are stronger, there can be no consistency in his work. He's like a partly trained athlete, what can be achieved one day will be impossible the next. And that's the way training goes. You should know that."

"I lose sleep about failing him, the thought haunts me and so does the idea of him hurting you in one of his mad moments"

"In a class of his own is Ganador," chipped in Sue as she helped herself to seconds. "And it's called extremely dangerous."

"But Ganador's not a normal horse, his ancestors were battle horses. As to his ability, well it's poor but getting better. Then there's the question of his past training?" Geoff leaned forwards across the dinner table and raised his eyebrows "Need I say more?"

"I worry about him … I can feel his difficulties and sometimes I wonder if Ganador can ever be improved by training, no matter how careful."

"You could try to be more positive, negative waves don't help anyone. Time to think about moving on, can't lunge him forever."

"Be a ticking time bomb, won't he Geoff?" chimed in Sue "Let's put that boy on him. You know - that would be groom. He'd soon find out what a circus is all about." And Sue started to laugh.

Sue, always laughed from the heart, one of those infectious, compulsive, giggles that spread to everyone in the room, and I knew the conversation had ended.

Why did other people's problem horses seem so mild when matched up to the violence of Ganador? On the outside he looked magnificent, but on the inside his spirit was of fire. A fire I'd never known before, that could raise its head at any moment, which smoldered with angry resentment. Ganador didn't live in any black and white world, he was in a class all of his own, a horse of King's … a battle horse of King's. Proud, defiant, explosive and highly intelligent- dangerous qualities in any man never mind a horse. Ganador did not fit in with theories; neither did he bend to rules. He was a horse from another time, a forgotten time that began somewhere in mythology…

I spent the next hour carrying out final checks on music. With a soft pencil I subdivided beats, sketched in missing fingering, and added bow markings. Can't be bowing up when everyone else is coming down. Can I? The music I'm reading through seems nothing like the usual stuff we play, from its very beginnings there's a hint of flamenco, a whisper of Spain. At first the idea is modest, even shy, and then the atmosphere and rhythmic pattern keep on returning, recurring, persistent, never going away. The surprise comes in the second movement with an oriental melody that allows me to see the whole picture, and then takes over the entire orchestra. It's hauntingly beautiful, with complete freedom of line and all the while the melody crescendos in an endless passionate swell. In a way, I'm reliving the flamenco from the Gypsy wedding…the music of the Romanies…a cry to join with the wind, wild and free, so that I don't ever want it to end…

Be interesting to see what the first violin makes of such irregular rhythms, let alone the passion. I wonder where the conductor found this one … holidays in Spain maybe. Even more confusing is where he found the soloist. Everyone knows that flamenco and classical make strange partners.

As I drove back home I reflected on the days happenings. The rehearsal had gone well, extremely well, and I thought back to the practice, and how in the second movement I'd felt a surge of pride. The only violinist to make all the entries! Another first - must be my lucky day.

'Thank God the soloists not here.' shouted the conductor, he raised his thumb above his baton, even smiled and he never does that. But how can he know, that flamenco patterns are stamped in the never to be forgotten corner of my mind? Like my shadow, they are always with me. For some reason I looked at the first violin, his face was purple with embarrassment. He who never misses an entry, came unstuck, obviously doesn't know his flamenco rhythms, not yet anyway. After rehearsal, I met up with college friends for lunch. They were organizing string quartet weekends in Ilkley of all places, which sound like fun, so I put my name down for January ... that's if I'm not snowed in.

Slipping onto the moorland road I drove slowly, watching a lone runner disappear in a shimmering cloud of mist. The very hardiest men ran on the moor, where every footstep was fraught with danger. Before the bad bend, I pulled off the road watching clouds racing across the valley ... five minutes of heaven from my high roadside terrace, minutes that I never could resist. At this point, the old moorland road separated two different worlds. On the north side stood the moor, bleak and abandoned but for numerous tracks and dry stone walls. You had to know the world of the moor from the inside to appreciate it. To the south and sheer from the roadside, plunged a softer world, the world of valleys and hills, of rivers and gorges. I gazed at mist rising over the damp moor, then hovering over the road...but only as far as the edge of the tarmac. Here, the mist stopped, as though a gossamer curtain prevented it from moving over the valley. As I drove away I heard the roar of engines. In single file two bikers roared past me. Not an inch to spare, accelerating madly as they pulled out of the bend. Heaving a sigh of relief, I watched them disappear into the distance. The locals called the moorland road 'townie run,' used as a fast shortcut from Lancashire to Yorkshire, or sometimes a race track between ale houses.

After the Inn I turned down the track into the farm yard. Switching off the engine I sat very still, just breathing in the atmosphere of peace and quiet, a serenity that had to be felt rather than seen. Through a haze of lavender light I watched Geoff lungeing Fred on the outdoor arena. The light was merely a reflection from heather on the hills as the sun dropped lower, but mysterious and fleeting.

For a few minutes I listened to his steady hoof beats on the hard sand surface, rhythmical and forward going, enjoying life once more after six months on box rest. And I remembered Geoff saying: 'breaks can mend in a horse and Fred's the proof.' Somehow I found it difficult to accept as true that Fred had regained soundness, especially after such a serious injury. Every time I watched his movements, so full of grace and agility, I found myself doubting what I saw and thinking only of the past. When he ran wild and free on the inner moor, a gypsy colt wanted by no-one, a threat to walkers.

"We've plenty of time," shouted Sue from somewhere in the stables. "I feel so excited!"

"Where are we riding too?"

"Devil's rock, so sayeth Geoff…"

Just after ten we rode south, down into the valley, through the gorge…over rolling hills. At the river we stopped by Willy's cave house to ask about the fox. He said it was the mate of an injured vixen living in his kitchen. 'He comes down every day just to check, he'll be getting her back soon.' At the top of the second valley we came upon a giant limestone rock standing sheer at the trackside. I followed Geoff up a soil path winding around the small cliff, higher and higher until we stood on its flat, moss covered top. The lights in the valley shone brightly, 'probably competing with the stars,' supposed Sue. Mill chimneys stood framed in silver against the glow of the moon, announcing their place in the family of things. The misery that once was, now only a memory … maybe a museum. 'How long can the blackness of despair cling to the fabric of any one building?'

'Look at the sky,' whispered Geoff, to speak louder than a

43

whisper might alter the beauty of such a perfect night.

'Wonder how many stars there are?'

'At a guess, many more than ten billion make up the milky way alone...'

'Why do I never see such a radiant universe in Leeds?'

'Probably light pollution ... a city isn't the best place for star gazing.'

'I've never seen the Milky Way so clearly.' Ganador stood unmoving, as I gazed at the mysterious pathway of stars arched across the heavens.

'What you really see is what went before, millions of years before ... the beginning and the end.'

The harvest moon rode high in the heavens painting the hilltops with soft white light, and I wondered if I looked at the last clear sky of summer...

*'Dwell on the beauty of life. Watch the star's, and see yourself running with them.'*

*Marcus Aurelius, Meditations 121 A.D.*

# *October*...Yorkshire Moors
## ...1980

# 5.  A Stack of Problems

The time was just after four p. m. when Geoff's car drew into the yard, the heavy rain was now a squally drizzle with an angry west wind blowing off the moors. In the distance I heard the howling of a storm and for the first time in months started to shiver. He dropped his overnight bag onto the cobbles in front of the farm and made his way down to the converted cow shed, the place he called his garage. I watched lights from the car flickering over the valley, and realized that every day would now be darker and shorter than the last. Even though only one week had passed since the rain set in, the carefree days of summer seemed a long gone dream. Summer … how I love the sound of this word. 'When mornings are golden and sunsets shimmer through a lavender haze.' But I must stop thinking about summer and get real, because this is the month of October the start of serious winter with its mists, torrents of rain and aching cold.

"Somebody's been busy." Geoff breathed in the scent of newly cleaned leather approvingly; there was no other smell so agreeably pleasant. He reached for a girth and slid his fingers along its silky smooth surface. "What's the secret formula?" he asked. "It feels spongy soft."

"Just hard work, the rain sailed down never stopped all day."

He walked over to the row of six mullioned windows, the ones looking over the valley and opened his arms for me to walk into. We stood there holding each other as if our lives depended on never letting go, just two kids gazing at the swirling mist clouds, the dancing shadows of dusk.

"Feels good to be home," his eyes looked tired and sleepy, can't help wondering if he's driven up from London with no stops, not even for a coffee or a sandwich.

"How was London?"

"Always good to visit..."

"What about the show?"

"Sports car section was out of this world, I'm glad I made the effort to see it. Horses all right?" Geoff loved the horses. He lived for the horses and the most important item on his agenda would be to give Ganador some liberty, some free time to do exactly as he pleased. For tomorrow he planned to begin part two of the stallions training, work under saddle and already I felt worried.

Early next morning the sound of clipper blades hummed in the yard as Geoff trimmed hair away from Ganadors nose.

"Scabs." he pointed to the lower nasal bone "Dropped nose band must have rubbed him. But what on earth are these marks?" Geoff looked puzzled. Small round black scars the size of nail heads were imprinted on his nose. The pattern of which could clearly be seen. As I ran my fingers over the marks I felt two areas of calcified tissue, probably where his bone had once been damaged. Tiny symbols of pain, of torment.

"Scars, caused by a studded sereta," I said with a grimace. "The marks used to be called a bracelet tattoo because they never fade away."

"Sounds like the middle ages to me, deliberate torture. Surely these things are not in use today?" Sue seemed shocked - she had a lot to learn.

"One or two may have stayed around, but in today's world a scarred nose brings the price down ... Although it could explain why he's got such a hefty bundle of problems."

"But why use them at all?"

"Some say it's a custom, like father like son, others think it's an easy to obtain submission."

"They certainly didn't break Ganadors spirit." replied Sue and I had to agree. But what they had broken was his trust in man, he'd become a rebel … the equine equivalent of an insurgent, ready to rise up and fight with his every breath.

I walked into the tack room and removed the sereta noseband from its pegs – the one I kept for display in the glass fronted cabinet. On the outside the leather was cleverly stitched, on the inside its metal had been neatly engraved. Just looking at the noseband caused me to picture 'Juanito's training yard,' a small yard in the campo of Jerez where I first watched the traditional method of breaking a horse, a place where the old ways meant the only ways. Juanito's yard was popular with the locals; it was on a road lined with cafes and bars which ran directly past its high walls. After seven p.m. the stables came alive with spectators, the voices of men and boys passing comments or applauding Juanito's antics. Also after seven, Juanito changed from a quiet, reasonable man into a bully. His routine was always the same, that of walking behind a young horse holding long reins attached to a studded sereta. He sent the horse well forwards with a crack from his driving whip, when satisfied as to the pace, he demanded a halt. No preparation, no word of warning, just a sudden halt. Once again, he would send the horse forwards, but this time his hands did not give. The horse met the full force of the unyielding metal noseband, a force three times stronger from the ground than it was from the saddle. Confused and fearful the animal tried to move on the spot, sometimes fumbling - occasionally offering a few steps of piaffe … the dance of the horse, but only the dance of the fully trained horse never the raw recruit. At this point the spectators went wild, clapping and cheering, the younger men jumping over the fence pretending they were matadors or bulls.

"Caballo baile!" they would shout "Buena- Buena."

If he was unlucky the horse reared, occasionally it put up a fight … for a short time. Easily bullied animals spun around or ran backwards, anything to escape the pain. Most probably the animal would rear or spin for the rest of its life, be identified as a difficult horse, all because of the actions of this one man. Never had I discarded these memories, they were always there waiting to return. I remembered the picture of a white horse, how I watched blood trickling over his nose, smearing his soft white coat with red - blood red on ashen white dripping down to his dancing hooves, before vanishing into the earth.

"Best not to watch..." Mum always said.

"I want to know what happens." I would reply.

"You should think of the bays, browns and blacks."

"Why should I think of other horses? The horse at the breakers is white."

"You can't see blood on dark coats ... but the horses still feel the same pain."

But surely times have moved on? Or is each country controlled by the rituals of its very own traditional customs? So that nothing except trivialities can ever change...

At midday I went into the school to watch Geoff ride Ganador. I sat back and relaxed enjoying the picture before me. Ganador had advanced a great deal in his trot work, his balance and rhythm looked controlled and secure - he was moving forwards more freely. I could now see it was possible to climb higher on the training hierarchy by aiming to capture just a little of Ganadors natural brilliance.

But suddenly the calm turned to chaos. One moment Ganador looked completely relaxed with nothing happening, and then everything started to happen together... before I could even think. The theme from Love Story played softly in the background, the work was simple, just changing across the diagonal in trot, from right to left and then vice versa.

On the feel of the right rein Ganador unexpectedly halted, threw his head in the air and refused to move forwards. Without any prior warning he changed gear into fighting mode, first he danced a rapid piaffe and then he reared.

"Get the whip-" shouted Geoff. Running into the arena I cracked the long whip close up behind Ganador. Upon coming down he kicked out with deadly accurate hind feet; so accurate that he snapped the lash. Chomping his bit furiously he moved forwards only to stop dead in the center of the school, where he changed tactics yet again. This time he hurled his body sideways into the boards. There was a crash, immediately followed by the horrible sound of wood slowly splintering.

"He's gone mad..." shouted Sue. She stood rooted to the spot alongside the balcony rails watching Ganador springing sideways, throwing himself and Geoff into the boards of the school. "He's trying to crush him," she cried out. "Can't you do something Norma?" But I was powerless. In his anger the stallion bounced off the boards. Running sideways, he slammed the weight of his body into the opposite side of the school.

As suddenly as the violent episode began, it ended. With heaving flanks he faltered to a halt, his mane damp and matted his body steaming. The fight was over and done with ... Ganador had tried everything he knew to defeat his rider. But his rider was still in the saddle and this he could not understand.

"Are you alright?" Sue ran over to take hold of Ganador immediately Geoff's feet touched the ground. Her voice was shaking.

"Am I alright? He tried to kill me-" Geoff's voice was faint he sounded totally exhausted. "Thank God I'm wearing these leather boots, and thank God I hit the wood and not the metal. Tonight, I'm riding him again, and in the interests of safety I'm stacking a line of straw bales close to the boards." said a disheveled looking Geoff.

"He lost his calm on the feel of the right rein," said Geoff.

"Will he ever trust that rein again?" I replied.

"Who knows? All depends on what happened in his past."

After his battle Ganador stood sullenly in his box biting his tongue until it turned blue. Sir Roland, Ganador's first owner had told me of this 'habit' of Ganadors, 'something I could never understand,' he had said. At that moment I conceded defeat, allowed myself to acknowledge that everything in life has a limit. Possibly Ganador had reached his limit, maybe Geoff had too, it was time to rest ... at least for the present.

I'd expected more than Ganador was capable of giving, at least for now. Gone down a path that might lead to disaster and it almost had. When re-training a horse with Ganador's stack of problems there could be no rushing. The warnings Fernando had given me were in fact startlingly accurate:

'Geoff should prepare himself for a repeat of stage one. Ganador is of the purest Spanish blood lines, and will possess the same natural abilities as described by historians, to carry out the same old exercises which made it famous, without any special preparation. And here lies the danger ... he will use these movements as evasions because he is afraid of moving forwards. Ganador has never been trained to move forwards, just held back. Try to remember he is the result of thousands of years of selective breeding, that his natural abilities are directly inherited from his ancestors, the same abilities that made the Iberian horse feared, once regarded as the finest combat horse in Europe.'

It was so obvious that Ganador had been stopped from moving forwards in any pace, except the ones of piaffe and passage. Until, through pain he had finally rebelled, fighting his breaker with every high school air he so naturally possessed, challenging the man who made him suffer.

And this was his story. But still the words of Fernando raced through my mind.

'Always keep in mind that you have time ... Ganadors problems mean you can multiply his sensitivity by x100 and still be within the realms of accuracy. He is a horse from another age, the age of chivalry and bravery. He is willing to lay down his life for his master. Today's equines are bred to be submissive even compliant to the wishes of man, no longer does he need the spirit of wild courage; the horse is used merely to pursue sport. You must also remember that he is not a young horse; therefore it is probable he is inflexible or stiff. My philosophy is to work him only for short periods and on alternate days. On the days he is not schooled walk him out across the fields. Ask little of him, together with free periods on his paddock. Remember the importance of kalm, for without kalm we have no horse to train, without kalm he is in flight - he is not listening. He has inherited the brave spirit of the fighting horse, you must have time. The physical and mental factors involved in retraining a horse such as Ganador cannot be rushed...'

In the days that followed Ganador was lunged or turned out onto his paddock, weather permitting. His lively spirit quickly returned and once again his whinnies and stallion cries pierced the stillness of the valley. Maybe I imagined it, but to me his whinnies were nothing short of melodious song … His very own song of the earth.

The temperature was now falling day by day, as it always did during the first week of October a fact that made turning him onto his paddock full of uncertainties. Ganador made his dislike of cold winds clear by smashing the wooden gate to his enclosure. Neither would he roll on anything but the softest surface, certainly not on the unpleasantly cold sand of a winter's day. But he needed exercise and quickly.

"Fernando may well be right," said Geoff as he examined the rock hard surface of the indoor school. "Riding him out could be the only way of keeping him fit, if you must keep to your alternate days." Geoff looked let down as he uttered these words. "Psychological scarring always takes more time, you should know that. Plus, he's not yet mentally ready to put everything together." But Geoff understood only too well that a different schooling routine was needed, if only to maintain the stallion's interest. "You could ride him out tomorrow, if there's no mist."

"I knew you'd meet him halfway."

"Long, long, ago I stopped pretending to myself that I could make a lunatic into a sane, sensible horse. If he's half normal you could plan to start riding him out down the tracks. But remember this isn't the Portuguese plains…it's the Yorkshire moor."

Geoff sounded more frustrated than angry. He detested being told what to do just when he felt he was on the brink of breaking through.

"I can't wait!" I said flinging a rug over Ganador's back.

"My advice is this … only ride on bridleways and make sure you always think forwards. Do not nag with your hands or his concentration will come back to you instead of thinking ahead." I allowed Geoff to continue with his lecture … he knew how important it was to understand the rules, that exercise and schooling had totally different aims.

"You remember the rules then?"

"I suppose exercise and freedom are essential if a horse is to be kept psychologically sound."

"And schooling and obedience make for safety. And you can't say you weren't warned…"

"How can you school him when his heads elsewhere?" I shouted.

"Return to something he finds easy. I had been thinking of cavalleti work, something to help him focus. Just remember that unschooled horses are like loaded guns–dangerous. And I don't want you getting hurt."

We both knew that Ganador was not yet ready to give even half his concentration to his trainer. So against our better judgment we put plan B into action, the development of forward impulsion on straight lines, or riding out. We would have to wait and see if this second approach helped ease the tensions of his troubled past; because until he relaxed we had no foundation on which to proceed. If plan B worked, he would become stronger and more relaxed, capable of showing consistency on a daily basis. Flexibility and calm were qualities worth waiting for.

Yet always at the back of my mind I worried that his unwillingness to move forwards may well be more than any stiffness, whatever Fernando said. But then, I thought of his words… words that seemed to have a way of filling me with hope.

'He may never give to you all that he wishes, but you must persist. Never lose the kalm, and he may then decide to trust you a little. When trust is restored we have a base on which to work … A little shaky perhaps, but sufficient'

After seven months on the remote Yorkshire moors, Ganador's physical health and beauty had improved beyond my wildest dreams. His magnificent figure resembled that of a statue, the only missing item being his chariot. He'd become stronger, his muscles firmer. There was no denying he was the finest horse I had ever set eyes on. Every afternoon at three I stood and watched him roaming free on his paddock, his hour of freedom, just him and the hills, such a magical sight.

"You look to be on cloud nine." said Geoff as he leaned on the fence "Trouble is," he paused and looked me directly in the eyes. "The stronger he gets the more dangerous he becomes. Strength equals danger with any untrained horse. And he is a stallion, he thinks of mares, territory and food in that order and don't you forget it…"

*'There are horses, and there are high spirited creatures*
*Fortunately most riders never meet the latter'*

*Fernando D'Andrade*

# 6. Valley of the Marsh Fox

*Diary, Yorkshire Moors, October 15.*

'For three days I've ridden Ganador out on moorland tracks, how I love the hours we spend on these long forgotten routes. The feeling of freedom and escape, when the day isn't preset and time is of no consequence. Riding out into the vastness of the moor gives a feel of living a dream. Nothing happens out there, nothing except the sound of the wind, which can be anything from a sigh to a scream.

On every track leading to the crags stand desolate farms. Many are skeletons, just part walls, a doorway, or a piece of roof. Long abandoned farms in the midst of bogs, with ghostly mist clouds whispering through shells of windows and doors as if trying to escape. There has to be a reason? Geoff tells me the vapors held down by the dampness of the bogs, I wonder...?

Yesterday, I passed a fenced off piece of ground where Gypsy horses grazed. In the distance I saw a peddlers' caravan with a stallion and yearling colt tethered outside. The stallion took my eye, though colored black and white he was a class horse and had that inimitable stamp of quality and spirit only possessed by the finest blood lines. In some ways he looked remarkably like my young horse Fred, found roaming the moors as a foal, and I reflected on the chances of whether or not the stallion might be his father? All the mares and foals had wall eyes and were colored black and white. So hungry were the animals they ate quickly and ravenously paying little attention to Ganador and stripping the rough pasture as if it were meadow grass. Despite being ignored, Ganador still thought his lucky day had arrived. Suddenly and with goat like precision he made a dynamic leap and jumped down a deep ditch, from which he refused to move. It took minutes that seemed like hours to coax him back onto the path. Immediately he realized the battle was lost, he put on a fearsome display for the wall eyed mares, which included a show of rearing and kicking out. I was lucky to stay on, and must remember never to risk riding that path again- if I want to keep him that is. When I told Geoff about the encounter he said 'almost lost Ganador to the gypsies didn't you?' and then he added 'once a gypsy always a gypsy - or so they say. Best keep your distance from gypsies and their horses - he's been down that road once.'

Now its October the color of the moor has turned to shades of grey - but there's still beauty to be found. Not a physical beauty, more a kind of energy, and sometimes I can feel it all around me. It's a place where past, present, and future all gel together, vast ... mysterious.'

On the fourth day, I followed a track behind the graveyard which led out to the moors wilderness. There was a light mist; it rippled in the breeze like ribbons of silver, always ahead, always moving giving a ghostly appearance to all I saw. The vapor clung to every stone, every branch, it encircled Ganador's neck, as if it were alive. Unexpectedly, I heard a woman's voice she stood outside a dilapidated farmhouse with hands on hips, leaning forwards to peer at Ganador. Taking a step backwards, she examined the brand on his left leg.

"It's the same white horse that chased me. I'd know him anywhere. Picked me up with his teeth he did. Look at my coat." The woman removed her tweed jacket and handed it to me. Like many moorland women she wore mostly men's clothes, cast offs from her partner or bought cheaply on Todmorden market. Her jacket felt warm and woolen, her baggy trousers were held in place with a studded belt. Practical clothes yet still she looked feminine. At the back of the coat I could plainly see a jagged rip under the collar.

"Can I pay you for its repair?"

"I've no intention of reporting him - or of taking money from you," she replied in a soft voice without a hint of anger.

"Carrying shopping bags I was, just walking down your footpath. Scared the life out of me he did!"

"Can I speak to your husband?"

"Eric never takes anything I say serious love." So I followed her into the farmyard where I found Eric seated on a wooden box, he held a hens head over what appeared to be a small guillotine. I watched him drop the lever ... A headless chicken shivered and jerked half way round the yard, it tried to flap its wings...

"Can't kill a hen with my hands..." he said. We all stood without moving, as the shudders of life slowly came to an end.

"Found this ere at a farm auction last month. Just lure them in...then chop." Thankfully, the hen's body had now ceased to move, it lay in the soil stock still ... a sign for the bantams to strut over and pick at the raw flesh. Eric chased them off by dropping the lever with a clang.

"I want to apologize for Ganadors behavior, I believe he frightened you wife."

"Wife lives in country not town Lass," he said sharply. "And this is what you get in country. Fact is, she's not a good climber ... Can't get over stiles, can you Mary?" Eric laughed and swung the sweeping brush at his bantams. Mary went inside the farm house and brought out tea and biscuits on a silver tray. After handing china cups round, she poured a cup for Ganador.

"Carlton told me..." she said. "Does he take milk and sugar? Well fancy that!" After his tea Ganador began walking backwards out of the farmyard, his signal for wanting to be on his way. What I'd planned to say had gone out of my mind, so I smiled and waved goodbye to the strange couple. Before riding away, I called out "Sorry once again." but no one heard me, mist clouds shrouded the farm - the pair seemed to fade away, just like a dream...

\*

The following day was clear of any hazy mist, ideal for riding in the foothills of Calder Valley. I followed the footpath which passed the half dead trees, and listened to the exhilarating sound of thundering water courses deep underground flowing onwards to the river in the gorge. Without reason or cause, the grey light of day became bathed in shafts of sparkling light, and green grass of the kind not seen on the moors gave way to soft valleys and fast flowing streams. I rode past fairy tale farm houses, with blue slate roofs where cows grazed in meadows and morning mists of pale green lingered round trees. I trotted Ganador to the top of a high rocky outcrop where I paused to look down on the town of Todmorden, known to locals as 'Valley of the Marsh Fox.' The old mill town nestled sleepily, deep in the base of Calder Valley, the area where the Industrial Revolution began, born by the hills and rivers around me, the life blood of all cotton mills, moisture and humidity. The pathways on the hills above Calder Valley were full of surprises, passing from wilderness to tree lined gorges, from hill country to peaceful trails around sparkling reservoirs. In each section of track, there stood at least two farms or cottages where people had never seen the likes of Ganador before. Who gazed at him in awe … or if they were brave walked over to be near him, and stroke his silken mane.

I rode home on a different track, where the river flowed quietly and the hills leaned less high. On rounding a bend, I discovered a footpath which led down to what looked to be a lake. As I followed this winding path, I came upon an isolated farm. It stood in a sheltered position, where low hills and a wooded area blocked the prevailing wind. The farm was unusual for two reasons; it had three stories and was built of York stone, always the sign of a gentleman's residence. At the windows pretty wooden shutters were painted sky blue and winter roses climbed round a high arched door, painted orange. I remembered thinking the farm must be owned by an artist, or someone with eccentric tastes, for not many people would dare put orange and blue together. Even though the month was October, the gardens shimmered in color, compared to the moor, and a brook murmured idly on its way down to the river.

The farm was called 'Cottage Whenever,' a strange name for a farm house. As I rode past the gateway I saw Carlton, he sat on a wooden bench with an older man. They laughed at the antics of bantams scratching in the soil, and sipped tea from pint sized mugs. The older man held a hosepipe, which he used to spray water on any bird unwise enough to stage a fight.

"Look who's ere!" Carlton nudged his companion with his elbow, "It's Lass from below graveyard on Spanish Oss, come to pay us a visit."

The older man walked down the footpath and held out his hand. He said, "My names Silas Thor. And you must be Lass from above the gorge." With his left hand, Silas stroked Ganadors neck, his right hand, he placed on mine. "I write about the moors and its wildlife."

"That must be fascinating."

"Oh but it is," he sighed. His sigh was soft and languorous, like the sound of a happy man. "I love my work," he said. "It's totally absorbing."

"Silas knows everything about Yorkshire moors," said Carlton. "Don't tha Lad?"

"That I do," replied Silas, without a shred of modesty. "I'm a geologist you see, and interested in the bottom of your land, the part where the rhododendron's plunge down to the gorge."

"You mean the boggy bit near the meadow, where the land sinks. Below water level it is. Never dries up. Geoff had to fence it off … the bog kept pulling the horses shoes off."

"I don't suppose you know, but the place you refer to as 'that boggy bit,' is one of the only areas left in Calder dale where the marsh fox lives in peace. Beautiful creatures they are."

"I never knew wild foxes lived near the meadow." I replied… and then I remembered the time I saw a fox, on its way down to the gorge, the way it flowed along the ground, so rich in color.

"Got a perfect diet they have-abundant supplies of hares and lambs and sheltered by the gorge. But have you ever asked yourself why your land sinks so low in this spot?"

"Not really, I imagined it might be due to the marsh."

"Did you know your farm once had a working gold mine on its land? Abandoned mine shafts sink over time, and rain does the rest."

"So it's not a bog … Are you sure?" Without replying, Silas hurried down the cobbled path and opened the orange front door with a push.

"I can see you don't believe me!" he shouted before disappearing inside.

"He's gone to bring map out." Carlton threw grain into a feed hopper, before firmly closing the poultry sheds door. "Foxes…" he said, as he went about checking the lock, "Can't be too careful."

"I had no idea about any of this."

"Well there you go, thav learnt something today Lass. Silas knows all there is to know. Writes fascinating books on moor and its history."

At that moment, Silas walked back down the path, he carried a large map, made of thick fibrous paper. I could see it was very old.

"Here it is!" he placed the map on Ganador's neck and pointed with his ballpoint. "Your farm is here, marked with an X. Directly to the front is Stoodley Pike. Now you've got your bearings follow my pen. Your land is at this juncture. Can you see the word mineshaft?" The mine was definitely on my land; right at the very bottom, on my favorite spot, where wild rhododendrons mingled with ferns. "I wouldn't mind testing the surface water down there and the stream in the meadow - with your permission of course."

"I never imagined the farm had a story to tell. Geoff will never believe me, especially when I tell him about a gold mine."

"That farm has a fascinating history, and there's been a lot of suffering in the making of it. A poor man's life was worthless when your farm went up. A good horse cost far more than any man. I could tell you so much about your farm."

"Do you happen to know where the oak beams came from? There must be over one hundred beams in the cottages and barn. I often wonder because there's no oak trees anywhere round here."

"Some of the beams were from slave ships in Liverpool docks. And if you don't believe me, look more closely. If you examine the oak in sections, its amazing what you'll find. Certain beams carry some poor soul's last attempts to say, 'I was here...I lived.' There's nowhere closer to hell than down in the galley of a slave ship. Five or more men to each long oar there were, with shaven heads and whipped raw by the lash. A man never lived for more than five years, some not five days."

"But how did they transport oak beams to the top of the moors? Some of the roof trusses are young oak trees."

"Horses and carts Lass. Hundreds of broken down horses were bought up cheaply. Dropped to their knees they did, pulling heavy loads up to the moors and back. Worked to death they were, and so were the men who did the toiling. Centuries ago, the moor was a busy place. There were tin and copper mines out there - coal too. Not many gold mines though."

"Lad thinks there might be a link between slave ships and mills. Inquiring mind has Silas."

Carlton walked over to Ganador; he said, "Bloody lovely aren't thee..." He gave him his mug to lick clean. "Plenty o dregs in bottom lad," and Ganador licked the bottom spotless.

"There could well be a link ... But we'll never know for sure." Silas folded the map and shook his head.

"Mores the pity," added Carlton pensively. "Silas found the same surnames. Slave shipcompany and mill owner both had identical names."

"There's probably nothing in it," said Silas. "But I've got one last question before you're away. Have you found the vaulted cellar yet?"

"What cellar, the farm doesn't have a cellar."

"Oh, but it does. And built from the finest stone in Yorkshire it is."

"We have searched, we've searched thoroughly. And there's no cellar."

"Look more closely Lass!"

"Inside the cellar there's believed to be an escape route - a getaway for highwaymen. Cleverly concealed it is, but I know it's there."

"Calm down Silas." Carlton placed his hand reassuringly on his friends shoulder. "Tha should bat for a long innings Lad. Thall put tha sen under weeds before tha time."

"That's where we all end up sooner or later…" I waited for Silas to go on, but it seemed his tales had finally come to an end. Pausing for breath, he took on the look of a tired man, as if the day's excitement had been too much.

"Better be away-" I said. "And you have my permission for testing, or should I say panning?"

"When gold dust bathes the meadow in sparkling light I'll be there." Silas spoke the words slowly, clearly enjoying the sound of every word.

"See you in early summer…" Reluctantly, I dragged my thoughts back to the present but Ganador had other ideas and refused to move. As soon as Silas ceased handing out sugar lumps Ganador decided to show off his skill in counting. Five times he struck the floor with his left fore, ten times with his right. At the end of his performance Silas beamed a smile and gave him yet another treat. Carlton stood and applauded. As a thank you Ganador displayed six strides of Spanish walk, a trick which made the two men very happy…

We left by way of a narrow footpath which adjoined the farmland to Cottage Whenever. Bramble bushes grew by the side of the pathway with bunches of glossy red fruit, hiding under clusters of tiny spikes. Wild blackberries, ready for the picking - the moors harvest of fruit, juicy, and difficult to get at.

The path ended close to the steep rocky head overlooking Todmorden, and again I felt a surge of excitement as I rode to the top. The view was magnificent; I gazed at the towering hills of Yorkshire etched against the skyline, watched mist flooding into the valley.

As I took up the reins ready to ride away I noticed a man standing at the opposite side of some large boulders. Ganador tried to rear, whilst singing out a challenge whinny.

"Hi there!" the young man said, still looking at the view "Just watching you dreaming."

"I love to dream." I admitted.

"My names Jav, short for Javier."

"Not a Yorkshire name is it?" The words just spilled out, I never meant to sound rude. Ignoring my remark he carried on gazing at the hills. Maybe I heard the faintest trace of a far-away accent, but nothing more. He didn't look from southern climes, his shoulder length hair was the color of burnished copper and his skin was fair.

"How come you ride a Spanish horse?" The man looked me in the eyes, and smiled. "Must be a story waiting to be told."

"How do you know his breed?"

"He's larger than life and carries the spirit of fire...How else?" The man laughed. "Or it might be that fancy brand on his flank." I was beginning to find this man irritating, he met questions with puzzles.

"So you know all about him. Where do you live?"

"I'm living with Uncle Silas... for now. But hope to buy an old farm. Seen one I like on the bad bend. Anything has to be better than living in Manchester."

"See you around then." I watched the man climb over the rocks and start his descent down the path.

When he reached the bottom, he shouted, "Sorry for scaring the horse!" I watched him turn and walk away; he carried a basket of wild blackberries...

In a few minutes the town of Todmorden was but a dream, vanished under a haze of clouds. At the withered trees, a chilly wind blew from the moors, and the once green grass grew course and misty grey. Halting, at the entry to the gorge, I gazed at rocky crags reached into ribbons of swirling mist. Dismounting, I loosened Ganador's girth, and walked by his side towards home.

"How's Ganador's new work coming along?" asked Geoff over dinner.

"He's enjoying himself, thinks the rides are great fun."

"I don't want to know about the fun. Is he bouncing forwards off the leg yet?" Sue stared at the ceiling. She gave a little cough then pretended to clear her throat. Geoff shook his head.

"Maybe he is, at times. But it's not a question of him obeying. He has to feel like it." Geoff smiled and considered his reply. "Sounds just like a ladies horse, they all say, 'my horse has to feel like it.' You can't wait for a horse to feel like it if there's a bus coming." So to change the subject I told him about the gold mine, wild marsh foxes and hidden getaway's for highwaymen. "Can't deny the land sinks," he said. "Foxes may well be living inside the old shaft … if there's any truth in it."

"Can we search again for the cellar?"

"I think I know where the entrance is. From time to time there's a scratching sound that could be a mouse. If I'm right, the cellars been walled up, plastered, and papered over for centuries. Provided you don't mind the house wrecked…I'll knock through."

Only two days later, I saw Silas in the farmyard. He stood near the stables talking to Geoff, with two students sporting Leeds University scarves.

"You expected me today?" he asked with a smile.

"I suppose I did and I didn't." I said as convincingly as I could. Maybe I'd misunderstood his words as to the timing of his visit. After all, he did speak in riddles.

"Can you remember what I said?" He kissed my hand and whispered in my ear. "Don't worry if you can't, only testing…"

"I remember every word, it sounded like a line from a poem and I love poetry. You said: 'when gold dust bathes the meadow in sparkling light, I'll be there.' That's what you said."

"And here I am! A tad too soon maybe, but can't abide all the waiting." Silas carried the sealed plastic covered maps into the farm house, fixed a light filter over the electric bulb, placed a special cover on the table and sealed the closed curtains. "Light," he pointed out. "Scourge of old manuscripts." After handing out special gloves, he removed the first old map. I gasped as he spread the old drawing out. Although faded, it looked like a delicate water color and showed a different valley to the one I knew. There was nothing of the bleakness of the moors, just a portrayal of lush countryside. A copse stood on the area of boggy land, broad leaf trees sprung from the banks of streams.

His eyes sparkled as he talked about the history of mining, geological disturbances and climate change … from as far back as the ice ages. How the erosion of peat had exposed signs of ancient forests - enormous tree roots found hidden in the acidic waters of bogs. How limestone was gathered and formed from the shells of tiny sea creatures, when the sea covered the land, from farther back than the mists of time … and how when the sea drew back, this soft rock was brought to land…a living, breathing piece of ancient times.

After his talk, he chose which areas to pan. There were three locations, the stream in the meadow, the abandoned mine shaft, and the river in the gorge.

And the end result? It was a breakthrough of sorts. Silas discovered a nugget of gold in the gorge, which on closer examination turned out to be a single link of chain, likely discarded from a necklace. But to save the day, low levels of gold were found in the meadow.

"Is it sensible to think of re-opening the mine?" asked the student who panned the gold.

"The cost of outlay means 'no' - unless regular amounts are found on a daily basis. You must remember, the moor survived on small mining exploits, usually family affairs. Most possibly, took what there was, although you never know…" Turning to Geoff he said: "Have you found the vaulted cellar yet?"

"Not yet, but I am planning to knock a hole in the kitchen wall."

"I know it's there … just waiting to be found."

Following dinner the following evening, we moved into the sitting room to watch television, or so I thought. With a flourish Geoff removed a painting from the wall and all was revealed.

"Look what I found…" He pointed to a hole in the wall. "Come and look!" I ran over to the opening. Light from a torch illuminated the entrance. Spellbound I gazed at a flight of stone steps steeply descending to a doorway of some kind. The ceiling over the steps was high and vaulted. On the opposite wall were two paintings of stagecoaches exactly like the ones in the Shepherd, and everything I could see in the dim light looked sparkling clean. Not a cobweb in sight.

"When's the big day?" I asked, feeling pure delight. Finding this old cellar felt like discovering lost treasure or looking into a secret tunnel and wondering what it held. Here before me, was my very own piece of history, 'just waiting to be found...'

"There's no rush, been walled up for centuries" Geoff was thinking of all the extra work.

"How do you know?"

"Horse hair plaster lasts forever ... many hundreds of years, maybe five hundred, maybe more."

"Why is each step worn away in the middle?"

"Clogs," he said. "Steel tipped clogs on limestone steps. Been up and down all day they have. I wonder why?"

Two days later, Geoff made an entrance, just big enough to squeeze through. In the darkness, we crawled down the steep stone steps. At the bottom, I held my breath as Geoff unbolted the door. And there, hidden away under the old farm, we found a cellar straight out of a history book. The cellar was circular in shape with a high domed ceiling. All around its walls, were set three levels of shelves, perfectly rounded and built in York stone. Only one forgotten item remained ... an empty bottle containing a hard deposit of what may once have been wine.

"And what of the getaway?" asked Geoff "Are we searching?"

"No, let's forget it ever existed, I think we've uncovered enough of the past. Some secrets are better kept..."

# 7. Zachariah

*Diary, October 17.*

'Already Ganador's fame is spreading; his effect on the locals can only be described as startling. Whole families stand outside their farms to watch him pass by and Ganador always puts on a show for onlookers. Sometimes he performs Spanish walk, other times a lofty air bound passage. An old farmer over by the crags said these beautiful words:

'That horse…if a horse he be, is a creature from the heavens…'
After lighting his pipe he walked over and touched Ganador's silken mane, just to make sure he was real! In these 'off the cuff' displays Ganador shows me how the old airs should feel, and performs the same movements that his ancestors were bred for. Sue tells me he looks stunning, which reminds me of the date, October seventeenth…

Today marks Sue's final fifteen days here. Feel down in the dumps about losing her. Mum tells me I can't stand change. "Life moves on," she said. "And you have to move with it or you miss the boat. You know what they say about time waiting …?" Mum has such a lot of common sense, a quality I've never really understood.

Defying all Geoff's expectations, riding out seems to be working a miracle. Ganador settled into his new routine right away and when he knows its trail riding time his eyes sparkle with happiness, as if to say 'this is fun just what I want to be doing.' Maybe Ganador can feel the healing power of the high places? There's just one problem … he reacts furiously when any motorist passes him too closely or quickly. Yesterday, he tried to attack a car. Kicked out at a passing vehicle with a deadly accurate aim, so accurate, he dented its door. Perhaps he's got road rage, or thinks cars are not allowed on the roads? There's another problem too … one that isn't getting any better. His small rears are more frequent and can be dangerously high. But apart from any problems, there's getting to be a connection between him and me - a kind of trust that helps me understand his ways, far better than I understand motorists.

David the vet thinks he's strong enough to start canter work, and already I'm feeling nervous because I know there will be one hell of a fight. Geoff knows it too, he said, 'there are many battles to be won and I'm not backing off now'. Thankfully he's postponing any training for one week … Here I go again, approaching a point where change is inevitable. But there's no sense in speculating on the future, none at all…'

Already, the weathers becoming unpredictable, only a few minutes ago visibility was clear. I could see endless acres of windswept moor to either side, but suddenly the breeze changed and mist from the moor swept across the road. It's the kind of mist that covers some things, but not others. How I wish I'd ridden on a bridleway. Right at that moment, I imagine Geoff's voice … it's as though he's riding by my side and giving me a lecture, 'risking your neck on the roads in fog is unbelievable. You don't seem to care.' I begin to wonder if I do care…

The mist made normal vision non-existent, but the road seemed quiet. For the next few moments everything seemed peaceful, and then I heard an oncoming car. What happened next happened without warning …

Brakes squealed and a car swerved across the road coming to a shaking stop under Ganador's nose. He stood up high, almost vertical, his hooves flailing over the car bonnet. I clung to his mane in order to stay in the saddle. The next thing I remembered was the groaning sound of shattering metal as he came down with a crash. Through a cloud of mist I stared down at the scene. I saw what appeared to be a lady driver, covering her face with her arms. I froze in dread; the kind of dread only felt when something terrible happens. Time stood still, it had no beginning, no end. Ganador rested his front hooves on the car with absolutely no intention of coming back on all four legs. His ears were pricked, and he appeared pleased with his performance, calling out shrill 'look at me' whinnies into the clouds. Helplessly, I listened to the tick of the engine, not knowing if the smoke over the bonnet was mist or engine smoke. When he slid off the car and stood on four legs the driver wound the window down and apologized. She assumed the cause of the accident to be her unpardonable driving- and in a way she was correct. I just felt so relieved she was alive and not injured.

"He's wrecked the bonnet of your car." I don't know why I said those words because her car had just driven into Ganador, well almost.

"That's a small price to pay. Is the horse alright?" the woman's voice trembled. I nodded … remaining silent, numb with shock.

When she drove away, I looked for the nearest bridleway. To my right was a deeply rutted soil track, the kind of trail I tried to avoid. The going was full of sticky mud, the kind of mud that loosens horse shoes, but there were no cars to do battle with. For a while I rode in silence; the only occasional sounds being the bleating of startled sheep. Suddenly and shatteringly, there rang out a deafening clanging noise, which seemed to originate from behind the stone wall immediately to my left. Ganador leapt into the air, and proceeded to whirl round several times, splattering mud all over him and me. He then tried to run backwards, thankfully without success, his progress to the rear being halted by a stone wall and the sudden appearance of Zachariah, who stood up from behind his wall holding a mallet and bucket.

"Didn't mean to startle oss … Just knocking bottoms out of these old buckets, amazing what they come in for." Zak stood motionless waiting for Ganador to be still, his weather beaten, honest face glowed red with embarrassment.

"Really," I said unkindly, as Ganador settled into a maddening piaffe. "I have absolutely no idea what rusty buckets are useful for…"

"Dost tha want a cup o tea Lass? Its calming tha knows." Zak took in my mud stained face and angry voice "How's about a carrot for his majesty ... To calm him down like?" Zak looked at me with perceptive dark eyes, that more than any other quality betrayed his Polish descent "Its mek tha mind up time Lass."

"Yes please ... if it's not too much trouble. Ganador loves tea." Zak did not look surprised. After thirty five years on the moors he possessed all the traits of a Yorkshire man, and Yorkshire men never show feelings.

"How's the oss about to sup his tea Lass? Thas a bucket oer there-" He pointed to a stack of rusty buckets hidden behind his stone wall, the very same ones that caused all the trouble.

"Ganador only drinks tea from a cup Zak..." It was then I saw a look of pure astonishment cross his face. "Some Gypsies taught him how to sip from a cup." His brow wrinkled in surprise.

"Does the oss take milk and sugar too?"

"Milk and two sugars please."

Zak was silent for a moment, before returning to his farm house for the required number of cups.

"Will this un do?" he held up a pretty hand painted china cup, the image was of a thistle and a rose, the Scottish, Lancaster boundary sign.

"What a pretty cup Zak. Whoever painted it?"

"Wife did when she were alive. Lass is down under weeds now, she's in graveyard down yonder." He stood at attention, feet together, and removed his cap for a while. "Lass would love it, bloody love it, if she knew a good oss was drinking out of her cup." Holding the china cup to Ganador's lips, Zak looked on in amazement as the stallion sipped his tea.

"On the day I bought him, the Gypsy woman begged me to continue with his daily cup of tea..."

"Real clever folk them Gypsies." he said wonderingly. "They may be humble, but they have it all up here, especially with osses." He tapped his peaked cap with his stick; it read No. 017... The remaining numbers had all but washed away. "Old Carlton will never believe me...never in a million years. Before tha goes Lass av a question. Thav heard about them two farms oer Tod way?"

"Can't say I have-"

"Carlton tells me they're full of ippies."

"I think you mean hippies."

"Well now, I don't really know Lass. But Carlton says I can't go wrong if I think of three d's. They dress peculiar, don't work, and do drugs ... Is that right Lass?"

"I've never met a hippy Zak, but Carlton seems to know a lot about them- true or untrue." And with that said, he wished me 'a cappin day,' and gave a farewell salute.

Later that afternoon I rang Fernando, not daring to mention this latest incident to Geoff. In a way asking Fernando was much less painful ... Fernando had no idea about life on the moors, no idea visibility could be clear one moment but not the next.

"I need some help Fernando, some advice..."

"Tell me why?" he said kindly.

"Ganadors rears are becoming dangerously high."

"With a horse such as Ganador there is only one training method for problem rearing and that is to remove confusion. We ask the question – when we receive the correct answer we reward. Geoff must walk at his shoulder and you are to ride briskly forwards. Immediately he obeys reward, then again ride briskly forwards and reward again. Together, you will learn the silent language of understanding between man and horse. When his confusion has ended, encourage him into a rear! And reward again. Later his rear will be turned into Levade. I promise, this is the only method to remove confusion. Ganador is a rebel because he was confused in his early training. You have probably seen so called trainers whipping the horse forwards out of a rear?" He listened to my answer carefully.

"Yes, I have seen whippings handed out to rearing horses." I thought it best to be honest with Fernando.

"And what did you think of the results Norma, tell me?" Fernando always planted trick questions into our chats, so I continued to say exactly what I had seen.

"Beatings seldom stop a horse rearing: some horses switch off mentally and ignore any beatings, others panic, becoming terrified of both trainer and whip."

"Exactly," said Fernando. "We have to remove confusion and teach the command! You must be patient and teach him to discover the reward for his obedience."

Fernando's extraordinary technique to prevent dangerous rearing worked like a dream, the stallion quickly discovered his sweet reward, and afterwards, would only rear out of piaffe - the beginnings of training levade.

Geoff's philosophy on the training was simple, 'Ganador expects to be rewarded. Clever isn't he? He can't see the point in wasting energy, no horse can. Especially wasting energy with no reward up for grabs...' Geoff said these words as though energy saving was a virtue in a horse, but maybe he had a point, perhaps it was.

"Thank God for present day insensitive horses that do not even think about pleasing their master or leap into caprioles at the slightest opportunity." Geoff meant every word, I could always tell if he was serious or not. "Riding would develop into entertainment, to be held in Rodeo Shows, if there were many Ganador's about." Geoff continued to concentrate on his cars for sale magazine. He sat in his favorite spot, back row of the balcony, his feet resting on seats. "He reminds me of this Ferrari Coupe. The advert reads, 'needs a loving owner, history of accidents and several careless owners.' Sounds like Ganador's past..." How he loved to have the last word. Unfortunately Sue and Geoff shared a mutual appreciation of childish jokes and Sue looked amused.

"I think you would trade him in for a Ferrari Geoff, I just know you would. I hope Ganador's not listening."

"No car dealer worth his salt would trade a Ganador in." Geoff continued enjoying his comedy sketch; probably for Sues benefit, as I did not want to listen anymore. I turned on my heel and walked away, but not quick enough to miss what he said next, "Far too much risk- unknown quantities always are- no history of regular services PLUS a faulty top gear!" Sue laughed out of courtesy. But

Geoff had a point. There was a definite problem with top gear; or in equestrian terms canter. Ganador had never offered one stride of this pace even when out free, which worried me. There were so many unanswered questions in his past, but what I knew, what I had seen, looked to be fear of breaking out of trot. And I had absolutely no idea how meticulously this pace had been banished from his mind, perhaps never to return. The time of discovering if Ganador would ever canter again was becoming near…

*Virtue shall be bound into the hair of thy forelock;*
*I have given thee the power of flight without wings*

# 8. The Coming of the Hippies...

*Toby Jug Farm, October 20.*

Fernando's letter arrived on Monday morning. The postman drove the moorland winter land rover into the yard, a minor detail, but one that struck the official coming of winter amongst 'off the beaten track' farmers.

"It's a package today love," he said with a smile. "Tha might have a present from Portuguese boyfriend." He paused, waiting for my reply, but something told me that whatever I said would never change his opinion.

"Got one here addressed to 'Baghdad Cottage'. Somebody in sorting must be playing a joke on me. As if Baghdad is up on Yorkshire moors."

For the briefest instant, I enjoy gazing at Fernando's bold script writing, wondering why he never allowed enough room for the stamp, forever sticking it on as an afterthought in the bottom corner of the envelope. I can't wait to read it.

This morning, I intend to read the letter alone, just me, the letter and a coffee sound like paradise. So I wait until the front door bangs and the sound of voices fade into the distance. Now I'm alone, I bank up the stove with logs, make a coffee and sit in my favorite armchair, the one closest to the warm fire. Before opening the letter I think of Sue, in ten days time she will be living it up in Spain, new friend's, new job. Sue will have forgotten about Fernando's letters and how she enjoyed them. Still, life moves on. Her world is moving on, just like it should do. My world is back on hold ... I can't get dad out of my mind. I must be going through another dark period when the memory of his voice keeps on breaking into my thoughts. It doesn't matter how busy I am, pictures of him and sounds of his voice just take over my mind. But if I'm being honest I don't want to let his memory go. Not yet. I prefer to have his memories, it's better than nothing at all. So I pour another coffee and start to read Fernando's letter.

'It is now time to develop listening and feel. In time Ganador kan listen to your thoughts and you to his.

His frustration on the right rein is normal and most probably caused by stiffness. My advice is this: never push your horse into resistance for self gratification for he will quickly become unsound, remember that you have time.

The right side and left side are as two unconnected worlds to the horse, what we teach on the left we must then teach on the right and from the beginning. This fact is predominantly strong amongst the Spanish horse, less so with ze pulling breeds. Problems are many during this period, stiffness, poor conformation old weaknesses – Thus we make the work easier for him perhaps neglecting the more difficult exercises working more on straight lines and less on his difficult side.

The rein must be changed often, across the diagonal and by use of the volt. Keeping the same rhythm is extremely important, the slower balanced trot should be used and then work on opening up the trot. Remember to keep again the rhythm, for a few strides on the straight line. Not always in the same place or perhaps he anticipates the movement and does not listen to the leg!

I kan understand the difficulties during the next phase of training, that of training the canter start, this will take patience and tact. You must never ask for this work if he is tired or agitated.

It will not be possible to urge him into canter by quickening the trot, speed kan only confuse him. Therefore we teach him the signal to canter out of ze walk or use the balanced trot.

*Not surprisingly he remembers his younger days, and the punishments he received for cantering, therefore kalm and time are essential.*

*The Iberian horse does not possess the effortless canter which is expected of other breeds. Iberian horses prefer to trot, as this pace has a greater propensity towards collection, piaffe and passage! This love of highly collected work creates great difficulties when used too early in training, and more so should the horse be broken for driving.*

*The more serious problems being knowledge of over collection; weak backs and loins as no muscles are developed. Not surprisingly few trainers will accept Iberian horses to retrain for ridden work!*

*I am at great pains to emphasize the importance of kalm as without this there is no training. His difficulties are mental and physical, therefore he will never be pressurized, but you have time! I hope you kan understand.... I have done my best.*

*'The Iberian horse in Europe, 'The Spanish Horse.'*

*The fame of the Iberian horse rapidly spread throughout Europe where his superiority as a combat horse par excellence carried his reputation to distant lands.*

*Not surprisingly the Kings and noblemen of Europe thought him to be the only mount for them. Thus the Iberian breed has had a great influence on present day breeds; used extensively to improve and upgrade native stock in every country in Europe.*

*It was around 1500 that classical equitation began to flourish as an art form. Movements that up to that period had only been used by the nobility of Europe quickly became known as ménage or school movements.*

*The key here was to train other breeds of horse to perform in the same way as the Iberian horse!*

*This is when teachers of riding or 'riding masters' began to rapidly spread through Europe. Riding Masters and academies teaching different doctrines as to how the horse should best be ridden and trained in order to emulate the natural movements of the Iberian horse. This to a lesser degree is still copied today!*

*The fame of certain riding masters spread quickly and so did their methods become famous as the best way to copy the Iberian horse in ménage movements through to high school. In this period the non Iberian horse's lack of flexibility and stiffness was not enough to spare him being put through the rigors of training , at least up to the standard of piaffe, passage and levade. Most horses not surprisingly were quickly broken down, their conformation and type being unsuitable for high school work. This is unfortunately still copied today although to a lesser extent.*

*If you think of the German horse, bred on flat green fields, with his straight back legs inflexible and unbalanced, he could not copy the Iberian horse's movements. Present day breeders having now realized their mistakes cross the German breeds with lighter more flexible lines. As many European breeds were used only for pulling, they tended to be heavy stiff and more difficult to ride. But this fact neither was enough to spare him the rigors of training. Again, and not surprisingly most of these pulling breeds broke down early, their breed and flexibility unsuitable to perform the Iberian horse's natural movements. At this point, many cruel lever bits and long spiked spurs were introduced to compel these poor creatures to perform high school work. Therefore the ability to imitate at least some of the natural movements of the Iberian horse founded the ménage movements of the present day. The purest Iberian lines are still born with the same natural abilities as described by the historians in ancient times and will carry out the same old exercises which made it famous. Movements inherited from his noble ancestors, the battle horse of Kings.*

*I hope I do not bore you!    Fernando... '*

Inside the bulky envelope I found a smaller package, with the words, 'Building Trust as well as muscle' written from one side to the other. At the top of the first page was a hand written note. The words stood out starkly, in bright red ink...

*'Remember! Always study the horse both mentally and physically to obtain good results from the training. Health, diet, strong hooves, excellent shoeing, care in stable. We place the horse in an artificial environment, and must therefore attempt to replicate his natural existence, albeit, as much as possible. The horse must remain kalm, balanced, and forward thinking, with light aids, steady rhythm, and enjoyment of his work! I think it is now time to introduce the double bridle, a little. Work from the floor on short reins. He kan begin by halting in balance, when he halts easily, the halt trot transition kan slowly be introduced. Later if the balance is good ze trot halt transition to include reducing the strides of trot. This exercise proves if the balance is good. You know it is important to have a light rein and maintain perfect rhythm, kalm and straightness. This work quickly leads to more collected work and will improve his balance. Now, you are building 'trust'... as well as muscle.'*

He then included a further eight weeks of training up to the beginning of collected exercises. As I read then re-read his instructions all thoughts of time departed, until I heard Sue in the kitchen and the rattling of cups on saucers ready for the eleven a.m. break. Feeling guilty, I realized that over two hours had elapsed since I opened the letter. Two hours spent doing nothing but reading Fernandos letter sitting next to a warm fire ... forgetting all about Geoff and Sue out in the torrential rain.

I was never aware of time when reading Fernandos words, what I learned was more important than the ticking of a clock. He told me of times gone by, when men were probably cruel, even brutal, and horses such as Ganador were ready to take them to the ends of the earth. He told me of the years when fighting horses were valued, and of times when all Europe desired their bravery and natural abilities.

*

"Anyone at home?" called Sue. "A strange man's waiting in the yard - wants to speak to you."

Waiting in the yard was a young hippy. From a distance he appeared tidy, even smart, all except for his hair which was swept back into a greasy pony tail. By his side, stood a very attractive girl, her auburn hair falling in soft waves down to her waist. The pair seemed out of place in a stable yard, especially one in the middle of the Yorkshire moors. The girls velvet dress tumbled almost to the ground; and both wore classy Afghan coats of the kind rarely seen on the high street.

"Original Afghan coats," whispered Sue knowingly, "the genuine gear. I wonder what they want..."

"I thought that hippies had been and gone?" Sue laughed at my lack of hippy facts.

"No way, rich hippies never went. There's been a gang down in Todmorden for years."

"What do you mean rich hippies? How can a hippy be rich?"

"It's a way of life Norma, if a hippy owns a trust fund ... so much the better. He can do more good."

"Or sell more drugs..." Sue looked away, my point ignored. "Maybe they know about the abandoned farms, the ones near the bogs?" And I remembered Zak's gossip about the farms in Todmorden, and Carlton's warning ...

At a guess, the man looked in his late twenties, the girl much younger, even younger than Sue.

"Hi there!" the man smiled, he held out his hand. "My names Ian, from the cottage behind the graveyard, and this is Amber." He spoke without a trace of an accent, his handshake firmly reassuring. "We moved in yesterday." He smiled apologetically, "Amber wants to rename the cottage- she prefers the name 'Baghdad Cottage' to

'Graveyard View.' Ian spoke as if asking my permission... When he said Baghdad Cottage, I immediately thought of the postman holding the mystery letter in his hand ... there just had to be a link.

"Call in for a chat whenever you have time to spare. I'm good with Indian teas, and Amber works miracles with eggs."

Amber nudged him, "Remember Friday and..."

"We have two market stalls; Friday is Manchester, Saturday Todmorden, but any other day will find us in."

"What do you sell Ian?" queried Sue, silently adding 'long velvet dress and Afghan coat' to her final shopping list.

"Handmade clothes from Afghanistan and Iran; thought I'd try to sell something of beauty, but I have to keep the origins private! If you need anything special I can always do it at cost price!" Ian smiled, Amber walked over to Ganador's loose box.

"I adore white horses," she purred, running her fingers over the stallion's silken mane. "This one has a magical charm, I can feel his energy." Sue could stand Amber's error no longer and decided to correct the girl's inaccuracy.

"You mean 'grey'. In the equine world, white, flea bitten, and dappled, are all lumped together and termed 'grey.' There is no such thing as a white horse... No such thing."

"But my dreams are of white horses..." Amber said distantly, ignoring Sue's facts.

She wandered around the yard staring at the horses and peering into the stables. "I've never been in a place like this," Amber said distantly, "where horses live in cottages, with doorsteps and fireplaces."

At this point, I knew I had to steer the conversation along cautiously. On the one hand Sue could be inflexible, sometimes downright stubborn. On the other ... Amber had all the appearance of a born dreamer, as well as a new resident of Moonraker Heights. I had to think of something to help the girls meet half way.

"Can you remember the story about the 'holy white horses' Sue? How they refused to enter Noah's Ark, because they were having such a good time playing in the surf? The Gypsy woman told me this inscription was found where the Ark was built:"

*'The foam from the sea spray,*
*As it touched their manes and tails,*
*Shining and glinting in the light,*
*From then onwards called white'*

"But they were Unicorns, not horses," replied Sue. "And anyway, it's probably fantasy." Amber, who up to now had remained silent, spoke up. I caught Sue's eye and lifted my hand for silence.

"I knew there must be white horses." Amber said softly, her eyes still closed. "What beautiful words..." she said, "Will you write them down?"

"I'll write them down and send Sue up to Baghdad Cottage tonight as postman." We stood behind the farm gate waving goodbye to the odd pair, watching them stroll up the track, back to their cottage behind the graveyard.

"Oh yes!" Sue whispered. "I'm visiting Baghdad cottage this very day. The wind doesn't often blow the likes of Ian and Amber in, does it Norma?"

"Well no it doesn't. But the funny thing is, I've never seen a cottage behind the graveyard."

"I have..." replied Sue.

"Where is it?"

"I think it's between the old headstones and the high side wall. It doesn't look like a cottage, looks more like a coal bunker with a roof on. Carlton tells me it's built half underground and used to be lived in by grave diggers."

"And now its Baghdad cottage, whatever next..."

"Well I think Ian's cool, and so are his coats."

On returning to the kitchen, Sue quickly spotted the package lying on the table, she looked surprised. "A letter from Fernando ... can't remember seeing it this morning. Can I read it later?"

I nodded and poured the coffee, "Didn't want to bother you

before you went out."

"This will be the last letter of Fernando's I will ever read ... makes me feel so sad. I'm going to miss his letters."

"And I'll miss having you to share them with." I said honestly.

"Don't say things like that Norma, you make me feel all sad. Think about my farewell party on Friday! I'm treating everyone to pie and peas, and I've baked a cake." Sue's high spirits were buoyant, excitement just bounced off her. She was full of the joys of seeing a bit more of the world, and who could blame her.

Sue's party was to be held in the Shepherd, a place not known for its comforts, but more for its echoing empty spaces, and bottom numbing chairs.

"Strange place for partying?" remarked Geoff, as he polished up a saddle "Full of stinking sheep farmers, hells angels and smoke. Still, it should be a night to remember."

# 9 Sue's Party

*October 24.*

On Friday evening, a large gang of Sue's friends turned out to see her off. They were newcomers to the delights of the local Inn and stood at a distance from the other gang, local sheep farmers, the men who were often called hill-billies. This was the land of the sheep farmer, only sheep could survive on such rough terrain, the ones that found freezing temperatures and storm force blizzards too difficult, perished along the way. It was a hard life for man and beast.

But on two evenings a week, maybe four in summer, these lonely men would meet up in the local Inn. Each and every one wore a bizarre uniform, of which baling band played an important role. Used for belts, shoe laces, or a stand in for missing buttons. The full uniform, consisted of army issue trench coats, that looked to be out of the first world war, army boots, and at least three pairs of old woolen socks worn over a layer of brown paper ... A moorland remedy to keep the feet warm. The rest of the uniform comprised of mud covered cap, half fingered woolen gloves and stout walking stick. To any stranger they must have looked similar to Victorian beggars.

The local Inn was exactly as it had been in the seventeenth century, nothing much had changed. It was seldom painted, and had few comforts. Its furniture could be called basic, oak trestle tables and hard chairs, all original. The Inn's flooring consisted of flagstones, with a sprinkling of sand. Any acknowledgement to the word comfort came from the warmth of the open fire. Through a haze of smoke it was just possible to recognize the original brass and oak bar, a special feature with pride of place in the saloon bar. At either side of the bar, there hung a tattered collection of old, greasy paintings. The scenes depicted the comings and goings of stagecoaches, all six in hand, all pulling either in or out of the Inns stable yard. Sadly the once proud stable yard had gone, been covered over with tarmac, belying the fact that long ago it was alive with the shouting of grooms, and clatter of hooves.

Not many people were aware of the Inns important history or former glory. For over three hundred years, the Shepherds Rest had functioned as a well respected hostelry. A safe place to rest, and change the tired horses. The narrow moorland road had once served as a vital arterial link between the cities of London, York, Edinburgh and Lancaster; formerly called the Kings Way, because of the carriage of mail, money and wealthy passengers.

History oozed from every stone and wooden beam, this was a place where highway men and passengers had once stood side by side at the bar. It didn't require any modern day comforts. Anything added would simply spoil its special aura. How many people would call it seedy; is anybody's guess. But I loved the unspoiled atmosphere and the friendly, if somewhat different, locals…

For whatever reason, lights were kept low in the Shepherd, at either side of the fireplace subdued wall lights whispered faint rays of gloomy light onto stone flags. Oil lamps shone softly from stone window sills. The only brighter light illuminated the till, the only daylight entered through tiny church mullioned windows, like arched slits in a monastery.

To the right of the fireplace, just past the alcove stood an oak door, less than five feet in height and completely curtained off with a faded tapestry curtain. Behind the door lay the ruins of a stone passageway which led into a small barn.

To step into the barn … meant entering a different world, a much sleazier world. The barn answered the Inns needs for a discotheque. Popular, even trendy with bohemian types, hippies, hells angels and anyone feeling playful - ignored by serious drinkers, sheep farmers, or those in search of conversation.

Inside the barn a cloying odor of damp and incense filled the air, with the addition of something heady and hard to define. The aroma seemed stronger in some corners than in others … satisfying yet at the same time overpowering.

There was no brightness in the barn, just a soft glow from lamps, one in each corner. A string of fairy lights hung sadly over the music system, odd looking people drifted past in various states of hallucinogenic trances…

The choice of music seemed to be left to the whim of passing dancers … rock, rap or mind mending.

Life within the barn had a reality all of its own, disconnected and detached from the companionship found within the bar.

'*To Each His Own*' had been written in script upon the stone pillar next to the music system. Carlton said it explained everything perfectly … 'us and them in barn.'

\*

On the night of Sue's party we sat close to the fire with Carlton, Zachariah, Val and David the vet. Carlton signaled me to follow him into the barn; he always had a quick look at the 'other place' as he called it. In the corridor that led to the barn the mullioned windows had been knocked out, it looked like a ruin. I could feel wind and rain … the place was freezing.

Carlton read the words out loud, 'to each his own,' before shaking his head and speedily returning to his special seat in the warmer bar, to relax in his very own reserved chair complete with velvet cushion. An esteemed client of the Inn, Carlton was respected by all. The uncrowned King of Moonraker Heights, Carlton embodied the three essential qualities of all true Yorkshire men, grit, fierce determination and plain speaking, which more often than not verged on impolite. At one time he'd been a councilor and possessed more than a little 'clout' with the powers that be. He had influential friends… Carlton's time was divided up more or less equally; mornings were spent at his moorland sheep farm, afternoons with his elderly mother in Heptonstall, and evenings in the local Inn.

"I wonder what the words in the barn mean..." I said. The meaning of the mystery words eluded me save for one thing... the style of script looked identical to the prose in the graveyard, the same florid style, the same artistry. "Maybe the barn served as a 17c morgue?" I said half to myself.

"Do we have to talk about morgues," said Geoff. "It's Sue's party."

"Lass could have a point Geoff," said Carlton. "My old Grandpa used to tell me tales of osses dropping dead on steeps as they pulled carts up full o bodies. All dead were sent up here, because that was safer for them down there. Tha might be right Lass. But changing subject, your Lass Sue looked to be enjoying herself. She never stopped laughing, not once. Good job she didn't come to Barn regular Geoff - if you know what I mean."

Carlton then began the all important procedure of lighting his pipe; it had to be to his satisfaction. With his stick he rapped out the rhythm of Mendelssohn's wedding march on the flagstone floor. Just the first two bars, never any more, and a hush descended over the saloon bar.

"Come on Lad, get on with it," Carlton hissed across the table. The first story of the night was told by Zachariah ... He always had amusing tales of life on the moors. Story telling made good money for the pub - it also got free drinks for the teller. Carlton conducted three beats with his free hand, and Zak began.

"Ministry man came up to see me last week." Zak's voice held a quality of suppressed glee, like most moorland farmers he was really a drama queen who would have been equally at home in a theatre. "That tea dinking oss at next farm could av done a better job, he were nowt but a silly billy ..."

"Shhh..." Carlton said suddenly "Londoner's are ere." Zak looked crushed, his story interrupted. The drinkers returned to the bar.

"How do you know whose coming in Carlton?" asked Geoff "Surely you can't see through stone walls."

"It's all up ere…" with his stick he tapped his head and waited for the front door to open. Slowly, the door opened with a long, painful, creak. Mist from the moorland road swirled into the Inn, it floated past the bar, whispering then mingling with smoke from the fire.

Carlton's eyes never shifted from the door, his stare fixed like granite on the unclear figures of Ian and Amber, who swiftly disappeared behind the tapestry curtain that led into the barn.

"Pretend not to look," said Carlton in a guarded way. "But Londoner's have just gone into barn. Nothing personal, but why do types like them feel the need to live up here?"

"Does it matter Carlton?" Zak paused, allowing time for the full implications of Carlton's warning to make some sense.

"Nowt matters if tha don't mind Londoner's taking oer Yorkshire's moors," replied Carlton. "Invading, that's what they're doing … My Dad would turn in his grave. Thall see it when it's too late."

Zak was unsure whether to go on with his story - he found Carlton's way of thinking beyond him.

"We are all ears Zak," said David the vet encouragingly. "What did the ministry man say next?" And a hush descended over the bar.

"Thav a lot more sheep than last year Zachariah', Ministry man said all official like."

"Bloody good breeders, I said. Count em if tha likes. They be oer near bog…"

"But is it safe to walk out to this bog, asked Ministry man?"

"Tha knows nowt about moor, dost tha Lad? I said. Full o surprises it is. Sucks thee down like. Good men and good sheep get lost to bogs, and I tell thee no lie. And he reached into briefcase, got form out and ticked boxes!" Zak roared with laughter, he could see nothing wrong with taking a few extra pounds from the ministry. He worked long days on the moor, he was worth it. "Old Carlton lent me his sheep for annual count…"

Keeping a few sheep or cattle earned the farmers slim Government grants, it didn't seem important that up to a quarter perished in winter blizzards, men died too … Surely the Ministry must know that any serious farming had to be impossible, could never be done on the moors...

"Dost tha not see why Lass?" Carlton stared towards me.

"You've lost me Carlton," I said.

"Double number o sheep gets double subsidy." Carlton patiently explained this minor detail to the half wits sitting around him.

"So you've had lots of practice filling subsidy forms in?" I winked and kicked Val's foot under the table.

"That's how I learned to read and write Lass, and I'm proud of it. We look after each other up here, don't we Zachariah? Thas got to be determined to survive up on moors." And I wished I'd never spoken.

"What I do for thee Zachariah - thee can do for me - and keep it under cap Lad." Carlton stared at each of us in turn. Bert behind bar brought over two whiskies and a plate of chicken drumsticks.

"Never heard a word," David the Vet quickly replied. "Protect thy customers has always been my motto."

"Quiet please!" shouted Bert behind bar. "Willy's next."

Willy Fox sat in a dark corner. Usually his fox lay hidden under the table but tonight he was alone. Willy had a gentle voice, a cultured voice which merged with the hiss of pulling pints and the hum of conversation.

"What's he talking about?" I asked.

"Willy Fox is talking about arsenic ... How it contains good and bad properties and why he puts a spot in animal tonics and a drop in morning tea." Willy Fox was an ex chemistry teacher who had to all intents and purposes 'dropped out'. He was also the moors hermit. Willy lived down in the gorge where he cared for injured foxes, most with missing limbs after being shot or trapped at lambing time. Carlton took care of him without making it obvious, the pub cooked his meals and never charged. David bigheartedly helped him with veterinary care, all freely given.

At this point Sue emerged from behind the tapestry curtain,

"What dost tha mates think of it Lass?" Carlton queried.

"They think it's primitive and exciting." Sue bubbled.

"It is primitive, but not like Spain," said Val. "They've not got their act together in Spain … yet."

"Tha won't get owt like this oer in Seville tha knows."

"But that's partly why I'm going - Hasta la vista!"

We walked home. Sue stayed in the disco partying, saying goodbye to her friends. She would probably be ill tomorrow. I didn't know what time it was, except that it was late. Mist from the moors shrouded the graveyard, mysterious and haunting. The pubs single lamp threw a shadow of light onto the stone cobbles. A distant whinny echoed in the darkness, shrill but melodic … There was just time to check the horse's rugs and give one last pat …

# 10. 'Wild Men'

*October 25.*

The morning after Sue's party dawned dark and gloomy- there were no landmarks…no hills or valley, the moor was cloaked in the cold, clammy mist of winter…and at every moment the sky grew darker. It was the kind of morning I detested, when staying in bed seemed preferable to yet another dark day. Geoff had fed the horses earlier, and then taken the land rover into town with a shopping list comprising of tools, and beer. Sue was still sleeping following her night of excess. I remember sitting near the window, coffee and toast positioned at my side just gazing out into thick mist, and wondering why the dogs were creating such a racket.

Then it happened…there was a shout, the tapping sound of steel capped boots, and two thunderous knocks on the door. I immediately thought the police were here - this was common in winter - walkers often went missing. Startled I ran to the door…Standing outside were two local farmers, both carried guns, and for a moment I stood looking into the eyes of the elder man, cold, cruel eyes. Both the men appeared painfully thin, with grey lifeless skin, and deeply furrowed features. I started to speak, but before I could utter one word the older man held up his gun and stopped me.

"This isn't a social call," he said shakily. "Tha dogs chasing sheep and I'm letting thee know I'm shooting bugger." His voice varied between a growl and a hiss - he looked down as if to examine his rifle butt. Not waiting for any reply, the men picked up their rifles and started up the path, the figures merging into a misty blur.

"Where's my dog?" I shouted into the mist.

"Black Edge - If tha wants to see shooting."

This can't be happening...Scamp, my miniature Yorkshire terrier, in reality belonged to Mother, and she was in Spain. Anyway Scamp always accompanied Geoff, he loved sitting on the passenger seat. And then I thought of the gossip in the pub about Black Edge Farm...If I believed it of course, 'Fanciful gossip,' Geoff had said. 'Ignore it - the guy had the look of a hermit to me.'

I began to tremble with fear, my mind felt numb, hands refused to work. With fumbling fingers, I threw on the nearest coat and ran across the yard. As I crossed the farm yard, I saw Ganador's stable door, it stood wide open ... with him gone. Filling my pockets with oats, I grabbed a rope and ran up the steep farm track before circling round the back of the graveyard.

Amber sat outside the cottage, painting a scene of headstones floating in the mist. "The mist kind of swirls..." she said thoughtfully. "Must capture the movement..." She smiled distantly, and continued painting.

I found Ian unloading Afghan coats, his van parked on a gravestone. "I need help Ian. They've threatened to shoot my dog at Black Edge Farm and Ganador's gone. I'm begging a lift and praying I'm not too late."

"Jump in ... right or left?" A short distance from the graveyard Ian braked. "Quiet..." he whispered, "the horse is there on the left. I'll leave the head lights on." In the glare of the headlights I walked towards him, calling his name and talking as if nothing had happened - telling him how his breakfast lay untouched in his manger. He whinnied softly to me. I lifted my hand to his head collar. At that exact moment a biker roared past, he was driving far too fast and there was little visibility. Ganador reared and kicked out at the blast of sound. I carried on talking even though I felt like screaming and held out some oats. He lowered his head to sniff my offering. I clipped the rope on, and breathed a sigh of relief.

"I'm taking him back..."

"I'll follow you down to the yard."

"How could Ganador unlock two bolts? It's not possible."

"I bet your visitors let him loose."

"Don't say that Ian - It doesn't help."

Ganador danced all the way back. Two blurry figures shrouded in mist, waiting for a passing car to obliterate them... I began to think I'd passed the track; but then I spotted the white painted stone at the top. After returning Ganador to his stable, I found the second lock, it was on the floor, its spring twisted and knocked out of shape.

"Let me see," Ian walked over, he stared at the lock. "The clips gone - he must have hit it hard."

"Can we go?"

"Stay calm, don't panic. Tell me the way…"

"At the top of the track it's right, and then towards the Steeps, the names Black Edge."

Ian parked in the farm gateway "Walk down the field- Keep away from the men … Your dogs probably hiding."

Inside the gateway stood a policeman, he asked my name, held up his hand, and said, 'Stop.'

"What the hell's going on?" Ian was getting close to losing his rag, his face had turned purple.

"Sheep worrying - that's what. I've given permission to shoot, and sensible thing to do is keep away." As Ian argued with the policeman, I silently opened the door and crept out of his view.

In the covering of mist, I walked over to what looked like a newly dug ditch, and there Scamp was … hiding in muddy undergrowth. Clasping him to my chest, I began to walk back towards the road, and the safety of Ian's van.

Out of the mist, four fuzzy figures of men approached me – all carried shotguns, and stared towards Scamp.

"Put tha dog down." A voice shouted. The men raised their guns - The police officer never moved. This was the rule of the moor…death to my terrier, he may be only cat sized, but he'd been in the wrong place at the wrong time…And now I was too…

"If you shoot him you shoot me…" I said with a sudden surge of fool's confidence. Now four guns were trained on me

"Put him down." A younger voice ordered.

"One more sound out of you..." I knew that voice, it snarled, it hissed.

I started to walk backwards, the mist swirled in ripples across my vision...The grass felt wet and slippy. My arms were numb, but somehow I had to keep moving. The crunch of bramble sounded like thunder on my every footfall, the faintest sound clear and nerve wracking. I felt like running, but that would mean turning my back on the shooting party. Only a few more steps, and then I should be close to the gate.

As I walked, shots rang out. I wondered why I hadn't been hit. A dog covered in blood dragged itself towards my feet... The dog tried to lick my hand as the men unloaded rounds into its body.

Suddenly Ian grabbed my arm, my heart jumped; he guided me towards the gateway.

"Keep walking backwards...Do not show this gang your back."

Two of the men followed, raising their guns menacingly. When we reached the gate they turned away, disappearing into the mist. The policeman stood between the gate and the van, he didn't say a word. His face said it all.

"Quick ... into the van, and don't let go of the dog."

"We'll get him later." A voice rang out. "The minute the vermin comes out of your door. He's a marked dog."

"Bloody natives, that's what you lot are." Ian screamed through the open window.

"Can't believe thall risk them pretty osses- Might just be in way like." The men began to laugh in eerie high pitched shrieks ... my blood ran cold. As the men laughed Ian started the engine and reversed the van down the track into the farm yard.

"Whatever are you doing?"

"I'm seeing what's happening," he said angrily.

In the farmyard was a scene of horror - four German shepherd dogs riddled with bird shot lay on the cobbles, as if dead... On hearing the engine, two of the dogs dragged their bodies' upright, in a vain attempt to get to the van.

"Let's get out of this hell." Ian accelerated up the track making for the safety of the road … only to find the policeman standing in the entry waving his arms about. Ian swerved left, forcing the man to flatten his body against the bars of the gate.

After turning onto the road… He quickly ran out of a never ending stream of expletives.

"Do you always swear in Arabic?"

"Always in Arabic - vents my anger much quicker. Anyway, how do you know Arabic?"

"Once heard … never forgotten." The words carried the same threat as a poisonous snake, venomous, on the edge of reality.

"Idiots have nothing to lose if they shoot us both. Used a banned sheep dip, and then poured the residue on the earth…found its way into the spring water supply. Two men are terminal – others are going crazy waiting…"

"What are you telling me?" I managed to say. "That we are all drinking poisoned water? There is no mains supply, not at this height. None…"

"Don't panic-"

"Could the poison get into our supply?"

"Technically no, water drains downwards. The village is higher…but Amber still insists on buying bottled water for drinking and cooking."

"How do you know all this?"

"Friend of mine in Tod-"

Suddenly I felt weak at the knees, thinking of all the horrific possibilities. He glanced at my shocked expression before carefully reversing onto a gravestone.

"A cup of Delhi should pick you up."

"Never knew your cottage existed…"

"Free parking and no neighbors- can't ask for more."

Behind the graveyard wall were three heavily worn stone steps which led down to a door, and here any similarity to a cottage ended. The interior felt like a cave, even a crypt. The walls were of stone, damp and slimy, the ceiling of oak … warped and out of shape, so low I could almost touch it. And I thought of what Carlton told Sue, 'probably been home to the local gravedigger...' I didn't want to imagine any further possibilities.

"Pleasant view of the moors from upstairs," he said. The steps were of stone - heavily worn in the center of each tread. "Past residents must have worn clogs, knocks hell out of limestone."

At the top of the nine steps was a living kitchen, its walls were lined in seventeenth century oak panels, all of varying widths and lengths - the exposed roof trusses were also of oak and gave a touch of style to the room.

Amber sat stitching sequins onto velvet waistcoats, her recently completed painting propped on the mantel piece shelf. "Do you like the painting?" she asked.

"I think it's lovely, can't speak for shoppers on Tod' market though."

"I guess I caught the movement of the mist." Her green eyes stared as if hypnotized, towards the tiny mullioned window.

"Did you find the dog?" she added unexpectedly.

"We found the dog." Ian muttered as he stirred the infusion.

I walked over to the window, to gaze not at the moors, but at a single brass plate, it read '1688-1696 Silas Son of Jacob.' The plate was set in the center of a wooden wall panel, at the side of the window ledge.

"Wonder what happened?" Ian stood behind me holding the tray of drinks. He waited for me to reply.

"Maybe they lost the body and used the brass plate for decoration."

"How can you lose a body?" Amber sounded shocked; her face had turned an unhealthy white.

"Easy, when there's a pile." Ian said with his matter of fact logic. "Whenever the low areas suffered disease or flooding, bodies were brought up here, by horse and cart." At that moment I realized I stood in the very same room used by the seventeenth century coffin maker, the same one as described by Carlton's Grandpa.

Carefully, Ian placed the three cups on a table. "There you go, always does the trick." The tea tasted of perfume and honey, almost immediately I began to feel light headed. Holding a chair, I struggled to stand...body swaying, legs heavy and ponderous.

"No-one knows where I am." My voice stumbled over the few simple words "Have to get back home..."

"I'll help you downstairs." Ian took hold of my arm, "Supposed to relieve stress ... must be the shock."

Scamp had stayed behind the front door, tail between his legs, shivering. As I lifted him into my arms, he softly whined, as if asking to be away from this room.

"If I were in your shoes, the dog would have to go. Remember what he said...a marked dog."

"I promise to remember Ian. How could I ever forget?"

"Before you go I've a favor to ask," he said in a whisper. "Best if you say nothing about our wild men. Stop her sleeping it would."

"Word of honor ... but she's sure to find out sooner or later."

"Better later..."

Outside the door, I breathed in the cool moorland air, retracing my steps I circled the graveyard and with a feeling of relief walked down the farm track. Still clutching Scamp, I walked into the house. Geoff stood in the kitchen brewing a cup of tea and buttering malt bread.

"Where've you been?" he said frowning. "My first morning off in six weeks, and what do I find. Horses not fed or mucked out, dogs going crazy, Sue in bed and you missing..." His attitude changed from irritation to one of amazement as soon as I told him what had happened. He looked at me doubtingly whilst I told him the story of Scamp and the poisoned spring water. "Sure you didn't imagine everything?"

"Ask Ian ... he witnessed it all. And he knows about the poison and the guns."

"Are you sure Ian didn't imagine it too? I mean, he is a rather eccentric individual..." Geoff could be maddening. I often wished he'd allow instinct or emotion to surface over his damn logic. The truth of this would out ... sooner rather than later, but at the present moment I felt too drained, exhausted and drugged to give a damn whether he believed me or not. After drinking a cup of sweet tea, the sleep I'd fought off so determinedly overpowered me...

That night I decided I had to know the truth - and the only way to acquire facts in Moonraker Heights meant a trip to the Shepherd and a chat with Carlton. As an ex councilor, he had more than a little knowledge of water rights, land law, and whatever else the council seemed suspicious about.

"Fancy a trip to the Shepherd ... to hear what Carlton has to say?"

"No way-I'm staying in. There's only one way though, whatever Carlton thinks, and it's to get the 'marked dog' away from here. Mum would have him back; she thinks the world of Scamp." Geoff spoke in his end of conversation way, the line of attack I hated, without a trace of emotion but so very rational.

"Surely you don't want that gang round here again...and keeping Scamp is rather like inviting them."

Carlton sat in his usual position; at the top end of the bar facing the door - called this spot his watchtower - never miss a thing seat. Through the smog he spotted me, he leaned forwards, raising his arm.

"Sit thee down Lass," he patted the next chair, and then continued to drain his pint.

"Nectar," he said. "Nothing better than a good pint..."

The difference between Carlton and the rest of the sheep farmers could be put into one word 'class.' Although he dressed the same way; lived the same life, here the similarity ended, he was always clean, shirts neatly ironed, boots newly shone ... with never a trace of mud. Carlton carefully placed his glass down and crossed his arms before speaking.

"Move closer Lass," he nodded to some local farmers who sat nearby. "What I have to say is for thee and thee only." The farmers moved out of ear-shot. When finally I looked at his face, I realized Carlton knew all there was to know, before I said a word...

"It's like this..." He hesitated before saying any more, as if imagining the scene around the isolated farm. "There's one or two bad apples in every sack tha knows. Lad's at Black Edge shoot owt that moves, if it crosses oer farm land. And as for walkers - old man's no time for them Lass, none at all. Footpaths and bridleways got fenced off years back."

"But the man's dangerous - He and his mob trained their guns on me..."

"Tha right there Lass - He's dangerous alright. Like a scared wolf he is. Not to be played with, if tha knows what I mean."

Pausing, he took a swig of beer, and closed his eyes. "But as for pointing guns at thee Lass, well nobody would believe that. He'd say they were pointed at terrier ... And Policeman brother in law would back his every word."

"You mean he's bent?"

"We call it family loyalty on Yorkshire Moors Lass." Carlton smiled at my off comer's lack of knowledge "Tha knows it's all in water then?" Shaking his head sadly he waited for me to reply.

"Ian told me there was some kind of an accident with sheep dip."

"Did he now ... So that hippy living oer in graveyard knows all about it?"

"He's heard rumors Carlton; this is why I'm asking you.

Are you sure-I mean completely sold on this water theory?"

"You can count on it Lass." He spoke in a whisper, as if afraid of being overheard. "When I held reins in Town Hall... there were spot checks done on spring water, especially round sheep farms. This new lot is nothing but a consignment of bloody fools - has no idea what goes on in countryside.... Did tha know it were me that drew Town Halls attention to all this? And dost tha know Ministry doesn't want to get involved? Say it might put folk off eating lamb."

"That's news to me." I nodded to the barman and bought his third pint.

"Tha should feel sorry for all them folks in farms lower than his ... Nowt happened yet, but its early days. Sheep have drunk more poison than men ... Lamb chops with a difference down there. A sad situation Lass - but with one good thing coming out of it..." He hesitated to give his next words more effect. "Thall soon be on mains water! Drain men are up to Black Edge now, but silly begger keeps filling ditch in. My advice is getting rid o little dog…If tha don't like guns that is. Some men up here are short o knowing civilized. I'm not excusing what they do - just giving thee a warning Lass. Wild men act on instinct not reason. Moors not all about scenery and solitude tha knows. Pity - but there it is … And keep all this under cap."

Scamp left Toby Jug Farm the following morning. Geoff arranged everything. There really was no other way. I explained everything to Mum, as soon as I arrived back from my meeting with Carlton.

"Send him immediately," she said angrily. "I don't want those nasty men anywhere near him." So I said goodbye … handed him and his documentation over to the pet courier, and returned to the house. In a way I felt relieved. Scamp would be happy in Spain with mum … and as Geoff pointed out, it was far better than being shot…

*'World's a stage for human life Lass*
*Some good, some bad, and most a bit o' both'*

# 11. The Hermit

*Diary, October 31*

'Tonight, the hills are sparkling white with frost and the sky is crystal clear - nights don't come more beautiful than this one. It's hard to imagine the dense mist of yesterday, when voices mattered more than faces, when we had to link arms and feel our way up to the Shepherd. But there's nothing surer the mist will be back. The only question is … how many hours before it falls?

The last Friday in October has finally arrived – the ultimate night before Sue flies away to Seville. It's the end of an era and the start of a new one, and in a strange way I feel pleased. And why do I feel pleased? Because it's been the longest six months I can ever remember. But I'll soon be finding out what the future holds...

p.s. Scamp safely in Seville with mum.

p.p.s. Geoff tells me tonight's a blue moon, the second full moon in one month.'

"Just look at the moonlight, the stars!" Sue put her hand over the switch to stop me turning on the electric, and together we looked up at the night sky. There was something magical about star gazing from the top of the moors. The moon glowed with a surreal brilliance, the kind of luminosity only witnessed in lonely places where there was no pollution and hardly any electric. I thought of what Mother used to tell me 'you need three things to appreciate the heavens Norma, pure silence, complete darkness and no people,' she couldn't have been more correct.

"It's the last evening stables!" Sue sounded blissfully happy as she contemplated the start of her new life. Whatever the future held she was embracing it, giving it a chance. How I wished I'd a fraction of her ability in accepting change.

"You're sure you want to go through with this?" asked Geoff cautiously "We're not forcing you to go."

"Of course I'm sure Geoff. Just imagine seeing the sun and never, never ever feeling frozen in bed. I could scream with excitement! Tomorrow I start my new life and it's going to be a warmer one." The moment she said 'warmer,' I felt a craving to live in a world where long johns, woolen vests and balaclavas had no meaning, in that other world of warmth and sun. Already the night time temperature had dropped to minus five, soon it would be minus fifteen or even lower. Every year the severity of the biting cold took me by surprise each year feeling colder than the one that went before. Moorland cold was merciless, it had icy tentacles that reached out to freeze and kill. Sometimes it stopped me sleeping, stopped me thinking. I suppose most people would call it a form of hell, maybe it was…I handed the night rugs to Sue, who considering her blue fingers looked amazingly happy.

"You may or may not be frozen in bed, but the sun brings out mosquitoes and other bedroom parasites." As neither Sue nor I could know if Geoff was serious or joking, we allowed his comment to pass unchallenged and pressed on with rugging the horses up, putting on warm fleecy night blankets in readiness for the cold night ahead.

"Just imagine," she closed her eyes and smiled, "warm, pleasant evenings sitting under swaying palms, sun in the mornings, sleep in the afternoons and all those designer shops!" I started feeling sad, for I knew life would be very different after tonight.

"Only toiletries to pack before I take leave of this cold damp country," she glowed with happiness, if that's possible. Excitement just bounced off her, whilst I felt lost in a last supper mood. "Promise to write long letters Norma. I'll tell you everything about the yard and the gossip. I will even write about the stable cat!" She laughed at my sad expression.

Suddenly there was a noise, the crunching sound of boots on frost covered stones. We stood quietly and listened carefully. Although we could not see him we knew Carlton walked down the track. He whistled his tune, just the first two bars over and over again, there was no need for greetings, for his tune said it all.

"Carlton's coming down the track," said Sue. "And I haven't put the drinks out yet." As he rounded the corner he took off his cap and held it across his chest.

"Av got sad news…" He looked down at the cobbles "Terrible sad news." His words seemed to hang in the air together with the steam from his breath, we all stood there not daring to move, just waiting to be shocked. "Willy Fox died this morning, found dead in bed…"

"Who found him?" asked Geoff "He looked alright yesterday."

"David found him; Willy called him out, said one o' foxes was in a bad way. But when David got there Lad were going cold. Had a note by his side setting wishes out," Carlton shrugged. "David did all he could."

"What's happened to the foxes," asked Sue. "Are they still down there?"

"Don't worry your head about foxes Lass. David took 'em down to Crag's, put em inside an old lair near river. He said he'll feed em for a time. Better off back in wild Lass than locked in a cage by some do-gooder…" Suddenly his eyebrows lifted, I'd never seen them lift so high before. "Thall never believe next bit o news." Carlton's eye's twinkled, his face lit up with happiness.

"Try me," said Geoff.

"Lad kept his money under bed … There were oer hundred thousand. Half's rotten with mildew, but David said a fair bits dry"

"Did he have a family?" asked Sue.

"No-one knows Lass" said Carlton "Lads christened him when he said he had no name, 'hermits don't have names' he said. So we baptized Lad with a drop o beer. He's been Willy Fox ever since."

"What's happening to the money?" asked Geoff, there was silence now, no one breathed. Everyone's eyes looked at Carlton; all ears listened to his every word.

"David's taking care o money. Half's going to a wild life charity and rest to be divided amongst his mates in Pub- after a good wakes paid for." His smile went from ear to ear, he couldn't help himself.

"And I thought he had nothing," said Geoff looking surprised. I think we were all surprised.

"Can't tell what a man's worth by looks alone Geoff. Anyway I'm nipping down there right now just to mek sure there's no animals left about." He looked at me and I knew I was going too "If tha coming bring cat carrier Lass. Promise there's no dead bodies about. Co-op has Willy."

Carlton's land rover was parked at the top of the track; he drove past the graveyard then the Pub and turned onto a scarcely used path. We drove down into the gorge, over the little bridge and past the half dead trees. The track was unsignposted there were no clues as to direction, none at all. On moorland tracks you took your chance as to where they led or didn't lead. After the river, he turned left onto an overgrown pathway hidden by tall reeds; he meandered right then left as he bumped down to the base of the gorge. Suddenly he stopped.

"This is it," he said. We were in a clearing by the river; there was no light, only the light of the moon which seemed to me to flicker blue on the rivers sparkling surface. "No electric down ere," he added. For a few moments I melted into this world of sound, the gorge was the opposite of my silent farm; it breathed in rhythm with the sounds of nature. Fast running water roared down from the hills surging over rocks then sweeping into the river. Everything around me had its own special noise, vibration and color. Mountain hawks screamed from cliffs, birds moved on narrow ledges, glistening skeletons of trees swayed over the river, gleaming blue in the moonlight. Ferns brushed against my fingers, the bitter sweet smell of a peat fire still lingered. But for some reason I felt afraid. Tucked under some large rocks was a door…

"Place is no more than a cave." He fiddled with the lock until the door opened. "Built into rocks it is." Carlton walked in and lit the oil lamps, one in each of the tiny windows on either side of the door. "Come on in Lass," he said. As I walked in a pungent smell made my eyes water "Foxes," he said, laughing at my fear. "It's not dead bodies. Willy's down in funeral parlor. Co-op knows how to take care o folks."

There were two rooms, a living room and a kitchen. A bed settee - rocking chair and table looked to be the only proper furniture, but the rest of the room could have been an artist's studio. Wood carvings in various stages of completion stood on the table, mostly of birds of prey, sketches of wild flowers adorned the walls, stones from the river lay everywhere, painted in shades of silver green, ochre's and delicate blues. On their raised tops, the stones were painted with flowers from the river and meadow, always a single flower, always wild.

Carlton carried a lamp into the kitchen - flickering light fell onto an old dresser. The shelves were thick in dust and not much more.

"Look at this-" He lifted a plate from the top shelf. There was a painting on the plate. It looked like the meadow, the magic meadow. In the center a white horse reared and pawed the air, untamed and free. It looked to be attempting to fly, just like Ganador did.

"Willy loved a white Oss," said Carlton. "Once told me that watching Geoff's Spanish horse took him back thousands of years in time, so far back he could see history."

"What a lovely thought."

On the second shelf, stood a few tatty old books, mostly encyclopedias, with a leather bound drawing book at the end.

"No harm in looking." Carlton handed the book to me. It was filled with sketches and notes and fell open at the heading 'sacred animals.'

"Read it out Lass- Willy would like that."

So I held the old book under light from the lamp and read out the first entry.

*'Thoughts on white horses'*
*'White horses have always been worshipped for their spiritual qualities. There's evidence that only white horses were allowed to pull the chariots of the God's.'*

*'Eight white horses were kept apart to pull the chariot of the God Zeus, in the time of Xerxes.'*
*'Sacred horses of the earliest civilizations were white; horses pulling the chariots of the Gods were white. Man has worshipped white horses for thousands of years. But present day man, still doesn't know why the figure of a white horse thrills him...with the exception of the Gypsies, a race which still reveres the white holy horse. Clearly, a legend as old as the hills, is still present in the minds of every man, woman, and child...'*

And I thought of the Romany wedding and the poem about the Unicorn's:

'Foam from the sea spray as it touched their manes and tails,

Shining and glinting in the light, from then onwards called white.'

Maybe it was all so simple really? Everyone loved a white horse, because white horses had been worshipped for thousands of years. Surely, it wasn't beyond comprehension to acknowledge that a speck of this magic was still deep inside everyone ... just like it was with the Gypsies?

"Clever man Willy were." said Carlton thoughtfully. "Well educated he was too. Could have made a few pennies with his handy work, knowledgeable tha knows. Told him time after time I'd get him a stall on market. Too late now though, too late..." Looking at the plate once more he pointed to the horse. "Very likely Spanish Oss," he said in a whisper. "Lad walked down by river in summer. Tha can see your place from down there. If it's not wanted I'll tek it home for mother ... as a souvenir." He looked to see if I objected...

I said, "You take it Carlton."

"Lad always had thinking cap on. '...wear tha brains out doing all that studying,' that's what I said."

"What did Willy say?"

"He said brains were made for thinking."

"I can imagine him saying that."

At the side of the dresser stood three covered dog baskets, sitting in one was a kitten. The tiny animal stared at me and its empty saucer. Carlton picked the kitten up. It started to purr.

"Be a good cat for stables," he said hopefully. So into my cat carrier it went, still purring and gazing adoringly at me … its next meal ticket.

"Got a name?"

"I'm calling her Suzy."

"I like Suzy," he said. "It's short and sweet."

On my return home, Geoff and Sue looked expectantly towards the cat carrier.

"What's in it - is it a fox?" Sue peered through the grilling in the basket door.

"It's a kitten … that's all."

"Does the kitten have a name?"

"She's called Suzy." I said "Carlton said it's short and sweet." As soon as Geoff picked her up she purred like a traction engine. "She knows this is her lucky day." Geoff carried her into the kitchen and placed her in the cat basket next to Boris, a young farm cat that preferred the house to the stables.

"Boris and Suzy," he said. "And Sue is going to miss all the fun. What will you miss most Sue?" taunted Geoff.

"Ganador, Fred and the dogs in that order…" Ram and Dan sat outside in the porch, sweeping the stone flags with their tails, listening to Sue's voice and awaiting their evening walk. Little knowing, this would be their last walk with Sue. "I keep wondering if Ganador might miss me. Get depressed or stop eating, because if he does - I'll have to come back."

"You can't be serious about returning to the ice age?" I said disbelievingly. But Sue made it clear that Ganador was the most important man in her life, right up to the day she flew to Seville …which happened to be tomorrow.

# SON OF THE WIND

*'Screeching hawks on ebony wings*
*Flying low oer gorge and field*
*Razor talons, hunting, seizing*
*Homeward bound with live prey yielding'*

*N. Jimenez*

**Piaffe, Ganador and Geoff**

**Courbette, Golega Fair Portugal**

Susan M. Triggs (Thomas).
1975.

Fred.

**Gypsy Fred**

**Donovan in Spanish Walk, Geoff Up**

# *Winter*...Yorkshire Moors... November ...1980

# 12. Shelly and Kit

*Diary, November 1*

'Still no mist, the morning is clear and bright. I can see shafts of winter sunlight sparkling on the south facing pasture, forming a haze of gold down to the meadow. Sue gave me one last hug this morning, as she pressed a gift into my hands. It's a lovely mohair twin set; the color's purple, the same soft purple as the tiny bells in the flowering heather. When the clock chimed nine, I stood in the yard feeling unaccountably alone, watching Geoff's land rover depart with one very excited passenger.'

On returning to the farmhouse, memories of the time I first met Sue came flooding back. I remembered our first meeting when she applied to my advert for a live in, 'trainee groom.' A shy pale eighteen year old with an oxygen starved look, consistent with living in classrooms and studying late into the night. I had watched her grow into a very independent young woman with oodles of self confidence. Suddenly, life seemed to have lost its sparkle - I felt depressed and lonely. Change always made me gloomy. Just as I was feeling sad, I heard Ganador's shrill whinny, its high notes pierced the morning air and I thought of the horses and dogs. Especially Ganador, who adored Sue, watched her every movement, listened to her every word. How could he understand the sudden departure of yet another trusted friend?

The following morning I cleaned out the grooms room ready for Michelle's moving in, attempting to give the room a cared for appearance. Sue's Spanish magazines lay hidden behind the left curtain, maps and sundry books, out of sight behind the right curtain. Finally I discovered hundreds of knitting patterns stacked under the bed, and retrieved a long convoy of knitting needles from their home under the mattress.

Knitting was Sue's hobby, her passion. When Sue watched television she would invariably be knitting, her pattern propped on the music stand, which stood on her left.

"Can't stand idle hands" she always said as she knit, purled or slip stitched, never glancing down. As if by magic the most beautiful work emerged inch by inch from her needles as she laughed along with her favorite television soaps.

"All done and dusted!" Centralizing the plastic flower pot I took one last look behind the curtains ... and my day dreaming stopped dead. Below the bedroom window a strange object floated high above the cobbles. It billowed on gusts of wind without form or color. Any chance of normal visibility had gone, closed off by a sudden mist.

Only a few minutes ago low cloud had swept across the sun. Vapor from the hazy clouds, fell like a silver film over the farm, steaming and rippling past windows, making vision blurred and unclear. I blinked and looked again, just to make sure 'it' was still there. For a second time I tried to gaze through the steam, and this time the object took on a form I recognized. It was large in size with the looks of a low flying magic carpet and it hovered directly over the farm house door. Running downstairs I opened the front door and peered into the mist. The dancing carpet seemed to be suspended in the air. It looked exactly like the top of an escaped float, the kind seen in processions. But there were no processions across the moors, not that I knew of anyway.

"Can't see for this fog - Is anyone there?"... A muffled voice complained from somewhere under the parachute. "It's Michelle ... Shelly! What a time I've had attempting to carry this damn thing across the yard. The wind keeps catching hold." In a moment of calm, Michelle seized a corner and together we coaxed the duvet down to earth and pulled it through the door.

"I'm so sorry to bother you like this," she said, gasping for air.

"But it was the only time mother could drop me off. She insisted I bring it. Mum said, 'you can't sleep without a warm duvet up there,' and shoved it in the boot. It's a tag fifty two, or is it eighty two? Filled with duck down which makes it warm in winter, but cool in summer…"

"Sounds miraculous" I said pondering on this statement. How any one garment could possibly be warm and cool at different times baffled me, though Michelle appeared to understand every word of the jargon about her duvet.

"Was it very expensive?" I asked carrying yet another bin bag of clothes to the door of her room.

"A present from a friend," she said cagily. "A good friend-" When she said 'friend,' she stopped in her tracks and tears ran down her cheeks. What I heard next, told a sad story.

Over a cup of tea, the tale of her treasured duvet began to emerge.

"Until last week," she said. "I had a boy friend. He worked as a diver on a North Sea oil rig. And 'this thing,' was his last present." She pointed towards the sad looking duvet which lay in a heap on the floor. "We went out together for two years, and only last week did I discover he's married, with four children."

"Who told you?" I asked.

"He told me. He said he wanted me to know that at the end of his contract he intends to return home to his family…"

"He sounds a real mean swine," I said. "You're far better off without him." Speedily, I handed her a box of tissues whilst trying to sound sympathetic. "Married men have a habit of returning to their families. It's their pot of gold - their worldly goods, call it what you will. If they need access to anything of value, home with the family is the route to take."

"But this was different, he never told me about a wife and children, I quickly became head over heels …" I filled up her teacup and gave her the last chocolate biscuit.

"My mother had a convenient name for married men whose sideline seemed to be misleading young women. She called them 'candy floss' men. She said, 'men who watch out for sweet girls to eat. Men of no substance…'"

Apparently, I said the wrong words, for Michelle's expression darkened like a storm cloud as she removed further traces of 'his' memory, into yet more tissues.

"The liar, the damn sod," she said. I poured another cup of tea, finding the ritual of tea making strangely calming, at least for me.

"Enjoy life - forget him," I said. "The worlds full of married men with children." Please calm down I prayed. I am not allowing you to run away … not on your first day. Suddenly she smiled, almost laughed.

"If he ever contacts me again I'll tell him to take his stupid gifts back home to his family - including this ring." She removed a cheap imitation diamond ring from her finger and placed it on the saucer.

"Working with horses is something I've always wanted to do."

"And a future in the R.S.P.C.A…" I added just to point her in the right direction.

"If and when I pass my driving test," she said broodingly. She stared at the duvet, then the ring, then the duvet. So I changed the subject.

"Let's carry this enormous sack of duck feathers into your room. A new start is about to begin!" And we carried the duvet yet again through the sitting room and up the stairs.

"It's just that I'm feeling a bit jumpy," she said, with an exhausted expression. "I was awake all night, thinking of my new job, my new life … that must be why." And so I helped carry countless bags into the groom's room. As Michelle turned to scrutinize the ornaments on the window ledge I speculated on why…

"Are you looking for something special?" I asked.

"I've just seen what I'm searching for," she said excitedly. Her eyes glinted and a pause for silence enhanced her words. "A good home for this thing…" She gazed at the sparkling ring for one last time before removing it from the saucer, taking aim, and hurling the 'thing' across the room… where it landed in the plastic flowerpot. "The pot on the window ledge will make a suitable home. It's my new rubbish bin."

By seven p.m. Shelly as she preferred to be called had succeeded in unpacking, seemingly unaware of her recent traumatic episode.

"I'm going down to the stables," she said, "to say hello to the horses and devise a plan of action." The moment she'd gone I ventured into her room, I could not have been more surprised. The room was transformed into a kaleidoscope of color; emerald greens, sunset reds, oriental oranges, had turned the once dingy room into a bright happy resting place. Hand woven cushions graced the window ledge, sequined Moroccan camel bags hung on the walls. There was a place for everything, and everything had a perfectly proportioned setting. The duvet was now covered by a crazy patchwork quilt, made up of orange silks and black velvet; it lay discarded in a heap on the bed, hopefully in its warming not cooling capacity.

Shortly before eight she returned to the kitchen carrying a book, its title: 'YOU ARE WHAT YOU EAT.' The words were large and crimson red, they screamed out a message to all who wished to live long healthy lives.

"I've been on a three week de-tox diet," she sounded extremely upbeat, "consisting of fruit, vegetables, and pasta. I feel much healthier already." Shelly said this in her very own inimitable style, a no argument sergeant major approach.

"Would you mind awfully if I prepare my own meals?" This was a statement of fact, not a question; a technique of using words with the aim of telling me kindly but firmly that she intended preparing her own meals from that moment in time. She sniffed the kitchen smells, hot fat to fry chips, melting cheese quiche baking in the oven, homemade toffee pudding in the steamer - but said not a word before returning to her book.

Something, about what she'd said or not said had made me feel guilty, and I began thinking about the contents of tonight's dinner… A three course meal loaded with fats and sugars. My cooking must smell terrible, at least to her healthy palette. Maybe, she could also sniff the sugary sweet syrupiness of the steaming toffee pudding?

Its delicious aroma was everywhere, reminding me of cake baking days when I was young. I had to admit that none of my food contained one iota of the necessary fruit, veg,' or pasta. My cooking began to appear suicidal; laden with a lethal cocktail of calories, and even worse, fats and sugars. Not a brilliant advertisement for healthy eating. Reaching for my diary I wrote a shopping reminder that went something like this:

'Pasta, veg, brown bread, fruit, must buy healthy food - as we are what we eat- according to Michelle anyway.'

Then I thought of the freezing cold and double digit zeros, the storm force gales that blew me over. Realities that seemed to squash any views on healthy eating, or so I told myself.

"Is Kit here tomorrow?" she asked, mercifully changing the subject away from healthy eating.

"He is - if you don't mind him about on your first day?" Secretly I dreaded her reply.

"Brilliant! I've stacks of work for the boy." She replied positively, in a manner I soon became on familiar terms with. How I envied her upbeat approach to life, nothing seemed to worry Shelly very much - not now she'd got over the boyfriend. Must be one of those rare individuals whose influence radiates calming waves all around her - who breathed order into everything she did...

Trying not to look surprised by her reply, I speculated on what the planned work might consist of. Compared to Sue's aversion towards the boy, Michelle's acceptance of the situation contained one very wide difference of opinion. Nevertheless, it was obvious there had to be some research behind her open arms policy. Any clever strategy requires careful planning.

"Always glad of a strong arm when straightening the muck heap or sweeping the yard." She revealed her plan of action without a hint of a smile. So this explained her line of attack - Kit was about to be downgraded to a farm worker?

Her statement was a simple observation of fact, brief and to the point. It held no pretence about training the boy, and little intention of allowing him near the horses or in the feed room. Michelle's plans showed uncompromising attention to detail and rock solid honesty. To Michelle, the boy fit into the box labeled 'handy man' or even 'farm laborer,' no less ... and certainly no more.

"He sounds a useful person to have around. Do hope he enjoys painting the tack room." And with these words she drifted away to her room, carrying one healthy looking dinner, perfectly balanced upon her all too thought provoking book...

Michelle started work the following morning, and after only a few minutes it became obvious she was everything I could have wished for. Stamped across her forehead, shone the qualities of any competent, skilled groom. She smiled cheerfully, worked hard, thought in a conscientious manner, and oozed perfect tranquility wherever she trod. Her nerves were of iron, and intelligence shone all around her. If I then add the virtues of patience, serenity, and lack of complaints; then Bob's your uncle, Michelle had to be the perfect groom. What more could I ask for?

As I watched her work, I had to concede that Sues 'old guy Xenophon,' certainly knew a thing or two regarding the merits of grooms, perfect or otherwise - even if he had lived in the fourth century B.C. ... or there-abouts.

As soon as my line of thoughts touched on Sue, the telephone bell rang in the yard. The ring had a determined, persistent sound, a continual, incessant jingle that could only be Sue. Dashing back to the house I quickly grabbed the receiver only to hear the anticipated voice of Sue: her tone of voice was breathless and gasping. She sounded short of breath, as if she were running.

"Norma, please tell me what to do. Please ..."

"Where are you Sue and why are you breathless?" I said, trying to sound calm.

"I've been stuck in a police station for hours," said Sue despairingly, "in a room full of cigarette smoke. It's terrible..." So Sue was under arrest after only two days in Spain? As soon as she could breathe - she told me the full story.

"I'm here to obtain a work permit, and whatever else requires stamping - but no one will listen to me. What should I do?"

"Listen carefully Sue," I said. "Walk over to the desk with your passport and letter of employment. Place in front of someone with a kind face. Say you want a work permit and ask how much it costs. It's something like, 'permiso trabajar cuanto es? If I remember rightly your Spanish used to be excellent."

"I'll try," she said, her voice returning to the realms of normality. "Some people are given celebrity status and get their papers stamped no problem, but the rest of us are treated like convicted criminals. My lines surrounded by police carrying machine guns and hand cuffs who appear to be guarding my queue," she complained bitterly. "If only I'd stayed in England."

"But Spanish police carry guns; they always have and always will." I tried to sound light hearted, but it was my entire fault - I should have warned her. "Tell me quickly how your Spanish is coming on ... Are you able to communicate?"

"It's terrible Norma, terrible with a capital T. I just do not understand one word of what they say. Having dinner with the family is a form of hell, we sit around an enormous table and everyone speaks Spanish - at least I think its Spanish." She sounded deep in despair, that melancholy desolation only felt by those unable to understand or speak the language of the country they live in. "But it's not the Spanish I learned..."

"But they will speak Spanish, after all, you are in Spain," I said rather unkindly.

"I feel such a fool. I learned hundreds of verbs but I never hear the one I know. Perhaps I studied the wrong Spanish? The words just go over my head at the speed of light, it's like electricity. They speak so quickly, running words together, rolling rrr's, making strange noises..." she sounded abandoned. "I feel stupid...I mean I feel stupid not understanding."

"Why not book a course in spoken Spanish? After all, you know a chunk of the written part, think of all those grammar books you studied."

"But why does my brain shut down when I know the words - or should I say verbs?"

"It's in hibernation that's all. According to Antony a fear of speaking other languages is peculiar to the English race, something to do with living on an island, or so he says. He thinks isolated civilizations inherit a shriveled language area. But surely you know the difficult part already?"

"Even so - I'm going to feel like banging my head on a wall for a few weeks. I know I am."

"Before the line goes dead tell me how many horses you're in charge of"

"I don't muck out or groom, or at least I am not obliged to; I tack up, bandage, lunge and put on rugs. Yesterday was a holiday and not one person turned into work, so muggings me together with Maria and son had to care for all the horses - sixty seven to be precise that I rugged up on my own. My shoulders and neck are cracking like fireworks and there are three enormous knots in my right shoulder. Promise to write soon and please send Fernando's..." Click ... and the line was no more. Sue's not having fun, not yet anyway.

Abruptly, the clattering noise from Kit's motorbike brought me back to earth with its nerve shattering din.

"Turn that thing off at the top of the drive," I shouted.

"Sorry..." he said. Kit smiled and propped the bike carefully against the barn wall. I knew I'd have to stand at the top of the drive to enforce this order ... or ask Shelly to give it. May as well admit it, my role as peacemaker between head groom and Kit, was no longer necessary; all peacekeeping responsibilities had been removed from my agenda. Michelle would give the orders as from this morning and I had no doubt that her passion for keeping things hospital ward clean would no doubt take up the largest part of Kits available time.

After only one hour the form of Kit sauntered over to the door.

"Norma," he whined through the window. "I feel bored. Shelly's too busy for talking, or so she said."

"Come in, sit down and tell me what you did at the circus." For unknown reasons these short breaks seemed to boost his spirits, restore him to his cheerful talkative self - before starting on his next cleaning duty...

Only one week later, there appeared a marked change in Kit's behavior. His grin had gone, his constant flow of chatter had disappeared, and on the right side of his face, in close proximity to his eye, he wore a hospital dressing.

"Whatever did you walk into?" I asked, wondering if the chimp had become more precise with his shovel.

"This is more serious than walking into something Norma," he said mournfully as his sorrowful eyes met mine. "I've been through hell... Do you have time for a chat?"

And so we walked up to the house where Kit sat in his favorite armchair staring at his hands.

"The woman tiger trainer attacked me." He spoke slowly, without any explanation as to why she attacked him.

"And what did she 'attack' you for, and with? Finally he looked up and began his story.

"On Saturday morning, everything was going so smoothly. Until the ring master shouted me into the tent. The circus workers were just finishing constructing the tiger cage, they were ready to carry pedestals in and throw sawdust down.

'Today is press promotion day Kit!' the ring master said. 'It's when we circus people display our professional skills in front of journalists.' He smiled and patted my back, and he never does that. 'I know I can depend on you Kit,' he said. 'To make sure our friends get good shots of Sheba...' Then he ordered me to climb up the ladder that leads onto the cage top. 'Be ready with the water bucket,' he said- 'Scatter some on the tigers immediately, if, they start hanging about. I don't want any fighting in the cage, not when photographers are here."

"Seems a strange thing to do," I said questioningly. "Throwing water on tigers ... are you sure you understood?" One of Kit's weaknesses lay in misunderstanding what he should be doing.

"I understood perfectly Norma. After the act, we throw water on tigers to disperse them into entry tunnels, otherwise they fight. Tigers don't like water. There's always someone on the cage top with a bucket." I was now becoming very interested in obtaining a true account of the story due to his defensive replies. Never, had I seen anyone holding a water bucket on top of a tiger's cage. And if I had - the last person I would give that item to … would be Kit.

He reached out for one of my magazines and sat staring at its front cover. And then he told me what really happened…

"I emptied the fire bucket too early," he said. And without showing any emotion he turned to page one.

"You did what?" I said. All of a sudden, Sue's warnings concerning the 'not with it' part of Kit came flooding back.

"To be fair, the tigers were all sitting quietly on their pedestals. I simply made a mistake. The water drenched her, completely ruined her head dress…" Kit smiled into the pages of Horse and Hound.

"Sheba was adjusting her silver bird costume in readiness for the photographer's. She looked incredible; dressed entirely in ostrich feathers." He sighed as though reliving the experience. At last I understood - He was thinking of Sheba's scantily clad body, leering at the bits the ostrich feathers left uncovered, neglecting his job when he emptied the water - onto Sheba.

"I had a bird's eye view from the top of the cage!! But the bucket slipped out of my hand," he smiled broadly. "The minute I saw what had happened, I climbed down the ladder rapid. As soon as my feet touched the floor Sheba stood there waiting, in a real rage she was, screaming and shouting."

"You could have killed me you silly fool," she screamed before she knocked me out. She had a punch like a prize fighter. The ring master told me I was out stone cold for ten minutes so he drove me to hospital.

I have two stitches where her rings hit me," he said pointing to the hospital dressing. I feel lucky to be standing here today; she packed one hell of a thump." He calmly carried on reading. It became obvious that he felt no guilt; in his very own words he had simply made a mistake.

"But Kit… you can't 'get things wrong,' around tigers, you nearly killed the woman. There she was, alone in a cage surrounded by wild animals, and you emptied a pail of water on her head. The woman trusted you with her life." I glared at him "Do they still want you over there?" but the answer I expected was not forthcoming…

"Oh yes, Sheba contacted me the day following to offer her apologies. She admitted going over the top," he said smiling.

"The show goes on!" He laughed nervously, placed the magazine on the table and strolled over to the front door. "Thanks for listening Norma," he said without a care in the world. "I feel much better now it's off my chest." I gave Kit one of my disgusted looks and followed him down to the stables.

Michelle was hard at work in the yard, just finishing grooming Fred.

"I'm away for a few nights next week," I said to Shelly. "Think you can manage? Geoff will be about to do all the exercising."

"Does Geoff know?" Kit broke into our conversation with his usual blunderbuss approach.

"Of course Geoff knows." I retorted feeling my cheeks flush.

"Just ignore him…" She carried on weighing out evening feeds. "He speaks without thinking, says the silliest of things… first words to fall off the end of his tongue. Don't you Kit?"

"If you say so Shelly," he said looking down at the cobbles, knowing that from now on - his comments were banned from our conversation.

"Going anywhere exciting?" she asked.

"Portugal… Its Golega horse fair, somewhere I've always wanted to visit."

"Lucky you – But where's Golega? I've never heard of it."

"Close to Santarem alongside the river Tagus stands a small ancient town, where the finest Iberian horses graze in its lush green meadows. The towns called Golega, better known as the Capital of the Horse… and every November it hosts the most wonderful equestrian show on earth, and this year I plan to see it…"

*'Every day of your life is a leaf in history.'*

*Arabic*

# 13. Golega Fair, Portugal

'Thank goodness I'm escaping. November rain storms began yesterday, the end of Shelly's first week. The rain sailed down in fearsome never ending torrents, crashing into window panes, shaking doors and flooding the pasture. Golega fair here I come...'

On the Tuesday I flew to Lisbon, where a blue sky and sunshine awaited. Manuel and Lourdes had planned some special Portuguese treats, 'sights you will never forget.' Little did I know I was to see the purest equestrian art, served on a hotbed of Portuguese culture - as unchanged today as it was centuries before, all due to Portugal's love affair with tradition and the Lusitanian horse.

After five hours flying time, the plane touched down, the engine sounds died away. The doors opened onto a bright new world... a world of light. As I walked down the steps, I entered a warm world with a cloudless blue sky and just a whisper of a breeze, paradise compared to the darkness of North Yorkshires moors. When I cleared passport controls, I made my way to the arrival lounge.

Manuel waited inside the airports swinging doors ... I knew it was him long before seeing his face. The glare of the sun shone brightly on his long rowelled spurs ... his wide brimmed sombrero pulled low and set over to the right. The strange thing was that Manuel never looked out of place. He made everyone around him look unkempt, as if they had purchased their clothes from the local market. This fact never ceased to amaze me, as did his clothes, his offbeat cowboy style attire of high heeled boots, tailored riding suit with bolero jacket, open necked white silk shirt and gold crucifix... not forgetting the highly polished spurs.

For a long moment I paused, and just gazed at his elegance, his magnetic effect on people and his irresistible smile. Manuel sparkled, as did his personality, he was larger than life, tuned to a frequency I'd never felt before. Possibly he was the last remaining Portuguese cowboy...

"Buenos Dias!" he said smiling happily. I had forgotten how charged his personality could be ... he kind of gave off electric waves.

"I am good Manuel... obrigado, e voce?" I stammered in my best Portuguese. In the midst of Manuels guillotine like hug, speaking seemed difficult. He began to laugh, couldn't help himself.

"Bien ... now you speak better Portuguese!" For some reason, he found my attempts to speak Portuguese extremely funny. Geoff said it was probably my northern accent that gave a strange sound to the pronunciation.

"Venga," he said. "It is good to see you!" In the late afternoon sun we slowly walked to his car. Manuel drove from the airport to his home in the Ribatejo region on the old road, which led through lush countryside, and past traditional whitewashed villages. He stopped only once, to show me his sisters 'windmill casa' which consisted of four levels, a ground floor circular kitchen, first floor round cozy sitting room, plus two, far above the ground bedrooms, all joined with a steep almost vertical winding staircase. The views from the bedrooms were enchanting, looking down on the sparkling waters of the Tagus. The river Tagus is the longest waterway in the Iberian Peninsula. Running from its source in East Central Spain, flowing through Portugal, where it empties into the Atlantic Ocean, and is regarded as an important part of Portugal's wealth.

Following our detour, we eventually arrived in Santarem, a traditional Portuguese town, with breathtaking views of the surrounding hills and meadows.

Manuel and Lourdes resided in the center of Santarem, their king sized apartment hardly large enough to house the collection of trophies and medals, won because of his genius in training horses. Though Manuel had now retired as a caveleiro, his well known skill in training bullfighting horses still kept him busy, reserving many hours of his day.

"He tried to retire, but the idea terrified him," Lourdes smiled then shrugged her shoulders. "And now he has more horses than ever..."

After unpacking, I learned the first 'treat' on my agenda was to be something called 'ladies afternoon,' a Portuguese custom held in the local bullring. Manuel knew my dislike of bullfighting but insisted we attend.

"The event is for you to enjoy," he said cheerfully, whilst finding two seats with the finest view of the ring. "It is fun and games Portuguese style!" As I sat waiting for the spectacle to begin, I started imagining cruelty in various guises, mentally preparing a quick escape route through the bullrings café.

Suddenly, a huge Iberian bull thundered into the ring, it stood in the center, angrily pawing the ground. To my surprise, a small senorita stepped forwards from behind the barricades. She didn't look like a bullfighter, not if her clothes had anything to do with it. She wore jeans, t-shirt, and carried a small cape. To my relief she appeared weaponless. The small lady made a few excellent passes to her forehand and backhand, encouraging the bull to come ever closer to her slight body. Manuel became carried away with the display; his eyes were fixed on each pass of the cape and charge of the bull. In between shouts of olé, he began teaching me the names of passes.

"There are three ways of tackling a bull..." he said without taking his eyes off the spectacle, "de cara - face to face, de costas-back to front and de cernelha- sideways on."

Spectators roared their approval, each pass receiving an earsplitting 'olé.' What happened next amazed me - the woman threw down her cape, grabbed the bull by its horns, and neatly vaulted over the surprised animals enormous back, an act which was loudly applauded.

That afternoon, I saw many senora's and senorita's showing

their skill with a cape, some making thrilling passes, others displaying athletic ability by jumping over the bulls back. After my initiation into this Ribatejo custom, Manuel said it was time to leave.

"You enjoy - te gusta?" he asked guardedly.

"Me gusta mucho....I loved every minute." I spoke truthfully, overwhelmed by his generosity in sharing a few of the Ribatejo's best kept secrets. What more could I ask?

"Then I am happy!" he said. And we walked up the steps to the entryway.

There was a man standing outside the café entrance; he waved and called out greetings. I felt sure I'd seen the man in the bull ring, dressed as a clown. If it was the same man, he was clever with a cape, always ready to attract the bull's attention away from the ladies. As we drew closer I saw that he still wore traces of the clowns make up...

"Why not stay for the celebration?" asked the man. "We drink to the brave senoritas!" Groups from the bullring spilled through the door, filling the bar area, then the terrace. Gay Latin music, sounds of chatter, clinks of glasses made me want to join the crowd. It was obvious Manuel knew the man by their friendly greetings; he introduced him as, 'my friend Rimo.'

"Can I stay here?" I asked. And Manuel promised to return within the hour.

In the café Rimo told me about his new horse...

"I bought him from Manuel, therefore he's very well trained, and perhaps you will see him tomorrow." He spoke perfect English, without a trace of an accent. "He is a good horse!"

"Do you work here, in Santarem?" Hesitating, he slowly sipped his wine before answering.

"I work as a mercenary," he smiled and said... "Don't look shocked." But I felt taken aback ... the thought chilled me.

"So things haven't changed much?"

"They never do-" He ran his fingers through his auburn hair, I felt sure he was analyzing my questions, wondering how much I knew.

Why was I surprised, because the date was different? In pre seventeenth century Europe, Iberian mercenaries were unmatched in the history of Europe, some say the world.

In the fifth century B.C. Iberian soldiers were in the pay of the Carthaginians, fighting in Sicily against the Greeks, fighting someone else's war. And Fernando's quotations came back to haunt me...

*'The Iberian soldiers, in the pay of the Carthaginians, fought in Sicily against the Greeks in the fifth century B.C. and, when they went to Africa...' Diodorus of Sicily, 40 B.C.*
*'At one time, mercenaries were exclusive to this area of the Iberian Peninsula...'*

Perhaps they still are I thought. Oh no, nothing had changed.

"Does your work take you away for long periods?" I felt out of my depth, I didn't know what to say.

"Yesterday, I return after six long months, but sometimes I work closer to home!"  He nodded, and then embraced me. I was beginning to dislike this man. "Don't worry," he said, reading my thoughts. "This job has never been my ambition. I'm a lawyer by profession, a damn good one. Now I collect information or ..." He stopped himself saying the next word. "The work pays well, better than any legal career."

"Are you sorry you ever got mixed up with the secret army?"

"Definitely not-" he said with a shrug. "Someone has to tidy up." Turning his head towards me he added, "No one knows what I really do - and I prefer to keep it like that."

After half an hour, the wine had almost gone. How I wished I'd stayed with Manuel, not been attracted by the music and chatter. Rimo leaned across the table to pour 'one last glass,' I could smell his alcohol laden breath on my face. His eyes were beginning to look red rimmed, possibly the result of nights or even weeks without sleep. If he'd asked me then, what I thought about his well paid job ... I would have told him to get back into law.

But he didn't ask, definitely couldn't care less.  He didn't look like a killer, but what did a paid killer have to look like? His green eyes sparkled, like a cat - I stopped myself thinking anymore. His smile looked warm and genuine, it was a kind smile, but was it one I could trust?

I remembered what Dad said when I asked him about 'taking out men.'

"Who trains these men Dad?"

"They're usually ex army men trained in espionage, and all that goes with it. The best ones speak a few languages, usually university types with no family, or ties. The proverbial loner-"

"How would I recognize one?"

"You wouldn't, they are always perfect gentlemen, have to be in order to do their job ... These boys are good at winning friendships."

There was nothing illegal in his work, every government in the world kept a squad of 'taking out' men. They carried out orders - that was all. But his words held a secret meaning, a meaning I could only guess at.

Suddenly, he started talking about horses as though our previous dialogue had never taken place, and I began to wonder if I'd been dreaming.

"Tell me how you compare the German school with the classical Portuguese style?"

"They can't be compared, at least not as equals. The horses are different. The people have bred a horse that suits their needs."

"Have you met other Portuguese trainers?"

"I've met a few..."

"Fill me in, I'm all ears"

"I travelled down to Malveira and then Cascais..." The group around me fell silent, for a time no-one spoke, the names held a meaning far beyond my grasp. Only Rimo looked amused, I felt sure he'd led me into a trap.

The chatter turned to quiet, the friendliness I'd felt only moments ago turned cold, or was it my imagination? Only Rimo smiled. A smile, I'd decided I did not trust. Why had he told me? At that moment I knew how it must feel to stand in a witness box ...

alone, without help. And then Rimo broke the silence.

"Where do you prefer Norma?" He strummed the table, and then he winked. I thought of Mother's golden tipped replies, her charm, and how she turned enemies into friends. 'But they are friends.' I silently screamed. 'Why am I thinking this way?'

"I prefer to be here of course." The moment I'd spoken everyone cheered, Rimo hugged me, I pulled away.

"Well played," he murmured. "I like your style."

"But what did I say?"

"Never mention names or locations; if you want to keep your friends. It's too early yet." He tried to squeeze my hand, which I rapidly removed, and poured the last drops of wine into his glass. Holding the glass between thumb and index finger, like the expert he was, he drained it in one go. "The country is still separated, if only by intrigue. Manuel is a good man, a brilliant trainer and my best friend ... he is a man of the people."

When Manuel returned, I heaved a sigh of relief and rapidly followed his every move. He had dressed in a silver grey riding suit braided with velvet, with the addition of a black sombrero.

"Now we prepare for Golega!" he said and everyone cheered...

*

Just before six we crossed the bridge over the river Tagus, towards the old town of Golega - better known as the capital of the horse. It's a small ancient town, in the heartland of the Ribatejo, where Soa Martinho fair is held annually.

The town is set in a valley, close to the gleaming waters of the river Tagus. And it is here, for the first two weeks in November that Lusitanian horses are graded, traded, and then sold to all parts of the world.

Manuel wanted to park close to what I imagined would be the town center. He drove through the suburbs of the old town coming to a stop in front of a row of lively bars and cafes, spilling over with riders, all wearing traditional Portuguese riding dress. On leaving the car I heard a familiar voice ...

"Hello Norma!" I swung round, and there between a hot chestnut stand and Manuel stood my old friend Maria.

"But I thought you were still …"

"In hiding," she finished the sentence for me. "I can't hide away forever-" Maria half smiled and shook her head. "Things are getting better…if only slowly."

"And how are the horses?"

"The horses are fine." She raised her index finger, maybe to indicate she couldn't say anymore. "I've brought the Andrade boy to Golega. I love Golega; it's the only place to compete, if you want to hear the opinions of experts"

"What about your land?" So as not to be heard, we moved closer to the hot chestnut stand. Maria owned land and stables close to Lisbon and during the unrest had moved her horses and self to the north of Portugal. I'd often wondered what happened to the land built on by the peasants, the half built houses, stolen horses … blood lines that could never be replaced.

"I had to stop worrying, had to stop throwing good money after bad. Legally, I didn't get anywhere."

"But what they have done is immoral."

"Maybe it is, but at the time there was no law against it. The peasants took a piece of my land, and the land was everything we worked for, but I must be thankful I still have the ranch and what little else remains." Manuel touched my shoulder, and tapped his watch, he pointed to the bright lights ahead. At that instant I saw Rimo waiting in the shadows, he was deep in conversation with a military policeman.

"I'll have to go… give my love to Enrique."

"We separated Norma, the strain became too much. I'm with Rimo now." I felt surprise and shock. "Rimo said he could protect me and the horses, I had to make a decision. Let's see how it works out." Almost immediately, I understood her unspoken meaning as to why. The Policia wouldn't be knocking on Maria's door now, not with Rimo about. He was much too important a player.

"But how do I contact Enrique?"

"The Embassy, we're still friends, we have to be friends when working together. Nothing's changed really. Rico lives in the Lisbon flat … Campo Grande."

"I must stay in touch with Rico," I said without thinking. Rico was always happy to lend a hand with any research, claimed he enjoyed spending lunch hours in Lisbon's museums, searching out artifacts and dates.

"Don't worry Norma. I'm sure we'll see each other soon." After saying goodbye we embraced, and once more I couldn't think of anything to say.

"Good luck," she said. "I'll be thinking of you…"

After leaving Maria I walked towards the stables with Manuel. Maybe it was then I fell under the spell of 'Soa Martinho'… Heard the hum of excitement and the haunting music of Fado, smelled the sweat of horses, and the heady scent of newly roasted chestnuts. All around me vibrated with an intensity I'd never known, so rich in color and atmosphere. Tonight was history, a look at times gone by, and now I understood the lure of Golega fair. Nothing could have prepared me for what I was about to see next. Around the corner from the cafes stood a huge floodlit riding arena, surrounded by crowds of spectators. I expected to see the center of the town, but this was nowhere to be seen, it had vanished. Had the heart of the town been reconstructed, as a rider's wonderland for the benefit of the Lusitanian horse, its breeders, and tourists? There were no shops, offices, or banks taking pride of place in Golega. This ancient town was the capital of the horse…unadulterated by modern day living.

Surrounding the arena was a track, where gleaming horses paraded, where Manuel would ride. Proudly, I watched Manuel enter, he rode a fully trained Lusitano stallion. It was black in color and carried the stamp of a purebred from the finest lines. Every few strides he halted to greet friends. The horse bowed on one knee lowering its head to the floor. Never, had I seen such grace or splendor. Golega would not be the same without Manuel … Men like Manuel were Golega. In his riding, in his person he allowed me to glimpse the legends that surrounded the river Tagus, dream like, obscure, just like the history of the Ribatejo...

Encircling the equestrian facilities stood exotic Arabic style tents and booths, each one representing a leading Coudalaria or ranch. Unexpectedly, I felt a wave of sadness for the people of this small, proud town. Their world had not moved on, its people were trying to preserve the old ways, but today's world had only new ideas.

Legends and myths, ever since the earliest days, grew up around the hills and valleys surrounding the Tagus River. The Celtici, a people of Lusitania, provided both inspiration and fuel behind ancient stories of the early Iberian horse. Frightening creatures, with hairy faces and speaking a strange Indo-European language that has never been translated. Possessing a natural flair for horsemanship, they were fearless warriors... believed to spring into the air from the hills close to the river Tagus. It is easy to understand how terrifying the sight of these men and horses must have been, when galloping towards the Atlantic Ocean, or towards the next battle.

These so-called wild creatures, worshipped rivers and streams and had an upper class of warrior noble. They were also famous for their many skills, including highly skilled metal work, supplied chariots to Greece and ornate armory to continents, including Rome. The Celt's were noted for their courage, daring, and suicidal fighting techniques, being famous as mercenaries from as early as two hundred and eighty three B.C. when Ibero-Celt's fought in Egypt. Horses bred in this region were believed to be the ancestor's of the Iberian Horse, today called Spanish, when bred in Spain, and Lusitanian, when bred from Portuguese blood lines. I stood close to the very spot where the legend, 'Son's of the wind' had arisen.

'Before Spain and Portugal parted there lived a herd of horses that could almost fly. They lived in the hills and valleys surrounding the Tagus, down to the old city of Olissipo, in the area known as Lusitania. The mares bred in this region were believed by some to be bred by the wind, because of their amazing speed and bravery. Foals bred from these mares were called sons of the wind.'

132

From the pen of Aristotle are the words: 'One does not see the wind, and the marvel of the wind can perform many wonders.' All these stories arose in the area known today for its breeding of the pure Lusitanian horse.

Trojan, Greek and Roman royalty once desired horses bred only in this area, the territory of the Ribatejo, near the banks of the Tagus, down to the Atlantic shores. And even today, there still exists a magical feeling surrounding this region, a sense of timelessness, an unreal, mysterious quality, something inexplicable.

"You will never forget Golega fair." Manuel could not have been more correct. I've remembered every moment...

*'One does not see the wind, and the marvel of the wind can perform many wonders' Aristotle.*

# 14. Trainer with a Difference…

*Santarem, November 4.*

On Sunday, I watched Manuel ride - but only after shaking hands with everyone in the packed gallery. Yet one more Portuguese custom I'd been unaware of, the almost religious devotion shown to leading trainers, especially trainers of bullfighting horses. Even the policia came in to chat and to marvel at Manuel's magic with a horse. He began the training with a four year old dappled grey Lusitano, which he lunged for a short time. Afterwards, he rode through figures of eight in a brisk trot, always allowing the horse to find its own balance. His training methods held nothing of the German school, his young horses wearing only head collars for lunging.

"The horse must learn to find his own balance … no side reins!"

Manuel established forward movement in various ways. "Sometimes by riding across country," he said. It was interesting to observe that his young horses already knew the aids for pirouette in walk, side steps, as in full pass, plus, a few steps of piaffe.

Manuel's next horse, in its second year of training, worked in all three paces, its schooling being aimed at improving balance through the use of frequent transitions, mostly in collected paces.

"The balance varies from one stride to the next. I control the amount of impulsion coming from behind- then regulate it with the hands. The rhythm must be like clockwork, before, during, and after a transition."

All Manuel's horses wore double bridles from the age of five, with no lowering or placing of the head. Work periods were short but demanding, Manuel rapidly changing from one exercise to another. With the more advanced horse, changes of pace were many. Within one complete circuit of the school I watched him move between Spanish walk, collected trot, rein back, counter canter, and a few steps of piaffe. Strangely he almost never used the circle preferring to supple his horses longitudinally, when he did ride a circle the pace was more collected. Manuel's horses never had time to think for themselves, he asked for much, but was content with little.

Exciting characteristics of the combat school remained in Manuel's riding, traditions and symbols which have become part of the classical Portuguese style. The symbol of the whip; was such a representation of the old school. Carried high, pointing upwards, as a lance would be, reins held lightly in the left hand, it signaled passage. Carried to the rear, over the horse's croup, it signaled piaffe.

Manuel carried a switch in both hands, when developing Spanish walk from the saddle. Once the hovering step of the true Spanish walk was obtained, he signaled the horse forwards into the rhythm of the soft passage, his leg aid maintaining the impulsion, the switch reminding the horse to 'lift his knees a little higher.' This unusual method of training passage out of Spanish walk, can still be seen in areas of Spain and Portugal, and is possible only due to the Spanish horses ability in moving from uncollected paces into extreme collection 'to gather himself together quickly!'

To finish, Manuel displayed his fifteen year old bull fighting stallion, with the intention of showing his mount and himself off! There were no judges to impress; this was a show only for the enjoyment of his audience. After working his horse on both left and right reins, I watched movements such as Spanish walk, Spanish walk backwards, Levade with crossed front legs, Pirouette on three legs, Pirouette with crossed front legs, one time flying changes round the school, finishing with a low spectacular bow to his audience. The whole performance was like a game to Manuel...

*

To my surprise, Manuel's show finished with a display of bullfighting movements. Unexpectedly, a boy wheeled a bicycle into the school; no ordinary one, its handlebars having been replaced by bull's horns. There was then a thrilling fight to the death with this bull-bicycle. I think Manuel won, for placing three bandarhillas into the velvet cushion placed behind the horns. When he had finished he jumped down and bowed to his audience, most of who stood clapping or shouting their approval. What I had seen, felt like waking up from a dream, the kind of dream you know you will never recapture. I thought of the words of Xenophon, on describing Iberian warfare.

> *'Iberian horsemen spread out across the plain, and galloping full tilt, hurled their javelins, if they counter attacked, the Iberians quickly retreated, turned, then hurled their javelins again...' Xenophon 287 B.C.'*

Manuel made much use of the sudden halt, speedy run, and swift turn, his transitions varied between advance and retreat, the very basics of Iberian combat riding - The Lusitano horse, the horse that is capable of carrying out these repeated maneuvers. And now, I watched the same combat exercises as in the time of Xenophon, right here before my eyes...

The day ended by seeing to the needs of the horses, followed by embracing everyone in the riding hall, included Rimo ... He stood by the door with a group of important looking military personnel. I was not surprised, they wouldn't let a man like Rimo slip through their fingers ... he was a class act.

At nine the following morning, it was time to leave the magical Ribatejo. Very shortly the exciting world of Manuel, bullfighting horses and the colorful people of the Tagus' hills and valleys would be but a dream. Manuel drove me to the airport, we walked into the departure lounge, checked my plane was on time, and then stood talking, he in Portuguese... me in English, but strangely it didn't seem to matter, we each understood the other.

"I bought you this - You like?" He handed me a sombrero, quite the most beautiful sombrero I had ever seen, wide brimmed, and lined in soft leather. The color was slate grey... the edging black silk. Inside the rim, were the words 'Chapelaria Miki Santarem,' my first ever designer hat. I put on the sombrero in exactly the same way as did Manuel, pulled well down, and set over to the right.

"How do I look?"

"You look lovely - E belo..." He surveyed me in a slightly amused manner, his dark eyes twinkling.

"Y para Geoff," I stared at him, not knowing what to say, and the dark Latin eyes looked steadily back at me. He raised his eyebrows in an enquiring manner. "Open!" he commanded "I buy from Golega-The very best."

Inside the box were a pair of long rowelled spurs, the metal finely crafted, brightly gleaming in the sun.

I'm not sure how I expected to feel when it was time to leave the magic of Portugal and Manuel... at the time it seemed like turning off a light, darkly depressing.

"Time to go Madam," the girl on the checkout looked at me uneasily; "flight to Manchester boarding now."

We said our goodbyes, and then I walked away, overcome by my own feelings.

"Buena Suerte Manuel, y obrigado," my last words disappeared under the noise of flight arrivals.

"Adios e hasta luego," he said softly, in a moment of quiet, before turning and walking away.

The sadness I felt about leaving Portugal, soon disappeared ... Life moves on ... The colorful Ribatejo now occupied a different world to that of my own. I was returning home, to a world I understood. On the plane memories of the weekend kept switching on like bright lights in a dark tunnel. Often, I thought of Manuels words.

'I give freely of all that I know ... What I show to you is from my heart...'

The plane landed on a dark stormy Manchester afternoon, the sky looked ominously low and unfriendly. Outside the airport, heavy rain was falling, and a blustery wind blew from the west, making the cold feel all the more unbearable. Home to good honest northern weather I thought. On the moorland road, conditions would be even worse - that was for sure. It was seven when I turned into the stable yard, just in time for a quick look at the horses.

Michelle had finished feeding and was about to put the final night rugs on.

"Has everything gone smoothly?" She tried to smile, but not cheerfully, she looked glum, so very different to her usual self.

"Did you enjoy the holiday?" she asked out of politeness. "Because it never stopped raining here - I wish I could fly away to somewhere dry and sunny." Shelly must have realized she looked tense, she turned away to fasten the rug. "It's this damn depressing darkness Norma, driving me mad it is."

"Know the feeling well ... I hate dark times." Nodding in agreement, I decided to change the subject. "Here's a present, a little souvenir all the way from Golega."

She gave me one of her surprised looks, turned off the stable lights then helped me take my weekend case down the path to the house. "What is it?" Impatient to discover its contents, she started running her fingers over the package.

"Open it, pretend Christmas is here."

She went to the table, carefully cut the tape, and then slowly opened the present.

"How beautiful – but what does the lingo imply?"

"It means... the Lusitano horse, son of the wind."

The gift was a painting of a stunning black Lusitano stallion, galloping freely across verdant meadows, and in the background there flowed the gleaming waters of the Tagus.

At that instant the front door slammed shut, and two wet dogs ran towards my chair.

"Sorry I'm late," Geoff shouted from the porch. "Did it rain all weekend Norma?"

"Nights were chilly, days warm and sunny." I went over to put Geoff's present on the table.

"How did it go?"
"It went quickly - far too quickly…"

After dinner, I sat thinking about what made Manuel shine so brightly in the equestrian world of Europe. There's so much I will never understand regarding his magic with horses, but there is no doubt that Manuel Sabino Duarte or Veca, as he prefers to be called, has the brand of a Master trainer. Perhaps a trainer with a difference, his style and skill having been adapted towards the training of bullfighting horses where instant obedience, courage, agility and intelligence are the sin quo non to stay alive when in the ring. He's a trainer who is not shackled down with theory; there is no rigid systematic method in his training. Instead, Manuel makes thousands of clues cooperate and intermingle until suddenly you see perfection.

His training aims are towards the attainment of lightning reactions, supreme impulsion and absolute lightness to the hand, a prerequisite in any top class fighting horse. Manuels training sessions include 'work without reins,' when he rides from the leg aid alone, his arms folded.

I have no hesitation in placing Manuel first as the most exciting rider I have ever seen, his horses perform as if free, man and horse moving as one unit. Watching him ride is to perceive the modern version of Gineta horsemanship, or ancient Iberian combat, as it once was in the hills and valleys surrounding the river Tagus, down to the shores of the Atlantic Ocean…

*'Cavalo Lusitano- o filho do vento'*

# 15. A Ride to Remember

*November 30.*

On the last day of November the rain eased, sunlight danced in luminous lights upon shimmering stone rooftops and ribbons of mist swirled around hills. When the mist lifted from the valley, I stared down to search for the lower meadow, the magic meadow where the hares ran free and a brook cascaded down from the hills. But the meadow had gone, not even its ghost remained. A lake of sparkling water now covered the lower pasture which only time and drying winds from the moor could return to its former grazing. I thought of Willy's cave house down by the river with its pungent smell of fox and sounds of screeching hawks. But now the river was high, the gorge lay underwater. For a time, it had gone, just like the meadow... just like Willy.

Throughout November the horse's had rested, their daily work out only a walk in the barn. But now seemed the correct time to begin the most difficult and frustrating training period ever; the pace of canter.

Ganador's training recommenced only after the blustery wind storms had fully settled, high breeding in a horse was never tolerant of the vagaries of nature, at least not with a man on his back. On the first day of mounted work I began to feel concerned as to what might be revealed.

"Geoff," I said, knowing this was the wrong time to voice any worries, but somehow I had to speak. "You do realize Ganador has never offered one stride of canter either on the lunge or free?" For a moment he hesitated, and then, he smiled placing his finger across my lips before impatiently replying.

"Shhh…" he said. "Words mean nothing to a horse."

"But there's just a chance the pace doesn't exist in his repertoire?" His gaze never flinched from the all important positioning of the saddle, checking of stirrup lengths, adjustment of girth.

"It exists alright; his brain shuts down whenever he thinks of the pace. My concern is his physical ability." Geoff believed in finding the source of a problem, not words … horses didn't appreciate words he often said.

"There has to be a first time for everything." He led Ganador towards the indoor school where the important work of relaxing both mind and muscles began. At the start of schooling Ganador was lunged, when ridden most of the figures were on the left rein with frequent changes across the diagonal to the right, exactly as requested by Fernando. When the stallion became resentful of the right rein, felt tense, or stopped moving freely forwards, a change back to the left or favored direction was swiftly ridden … Maintain the rhythm … Keep the forward movement, nothing else mattered when warming up.

Ganador looked strong and well, his top line rippled with newly formed muscle. There was no evidence of his once skeletal frame, which only eight months ago had filled me with despair. The improvement in Ganador's physique was more than satisfactory, it was exciting, and so were the glimpses of what may be possible with further training.

The mystery of his absent canter would shortly be understood. Maybe the cause lay in his early driving training … Or had he just reached the end of his physical ability? As I watched and waited everything seemed to be going wrong and I asked myself 'does it really matter if he canters? I wanted to stop the work, before I knew the answer. But it was too late…

"Here we go," said Geoff, he tactfully applied the canter aid, inside leg on the girth, outside leg behind the girth. My heart missed a beat as I waited for the fireworks to start. Ganador swished his tail and lengthened his trot stride. In the next corner Geoff asked him again, this time the stallion looked surprised, he answered by floating into a left half pass. The third attempt was on the left circle.

Chomping the bit furiously he moved with tense irregular strides, he answered by a transition into passage. Ganador had replied to Geoff's request. His reply simple to comprehend, a definite 'not one step.'

All the stallion's problems emerged large and dynamic just like his personality. There would be no canter. Experience had taught him that it was inadvisable to move out of trot. He remembered the vicious punishments for each and every canter stride taken, and he was sullenly determined not to co-operate. Courage and cunning were bred in him - Ganador fought to win and a fight looked unavoidable.

And then it happened, he erupted in a frenzy of rage … Coiling his body as a spring he jumped high into the air as though attempting to fly. Ganador was cantering without moving forwards, he cantered on the spot, his bounds upwards, gaining no ground forwards, his movements of the air and amazing to see.

Geoff quickly changed his position to that of a rodeo rider, leaning forwards, then back. His balance had to change as swiftly as the stallions. He must stay in the saddle, however violent the horse became.

Dripping in sweat Ganador halted, his black eyes looked away, he anticipated punishment. A punishment he remembered to be brutal. Quickly Geoff dismounted and placed a warm rug over the wet trembling body of the stallion, he said 'easy boy … you've done just fine.'

"Canter or not, Ganador will always be the most beautiful horse in my life." Michelle said flatly, her voice had lost its usual sparkle. She spoke scathingly, and made me question my motives. "I can't stand this training nonsense. Is it absolutely necessary to put him through this mental trauma, does it really matter if he canters?"

"Of course it matters-" Geoff sounded furious. "This is called progress. Progress equals improvement- and improvement means helping him forget his past restraint, teaching him that he can move forwards. In training we either move forwards or backwards. And he's fighting because he does not understand my question. As yet…"

"I'm taking him into the washing yard, coming Shelly?" Inwardly I sighed, realizing just how much she had to learn. I could only hope she understood Geoff's little outburst and the terrified eyes of Ganador …

Later that evening I went into my study to find the letter Fernando had written about Ganador's missing pace.

*'In Spain high class carriage horses rarely canter! It is not surprising he has no wish to use the pace again. He remembers the pain of his past experiences when every stride of canter would be punished. And now you are teaching him rules from a different book, where the main objective is to go forwards without restraint. This will take time and much patience. But you must learn that you always have time and constantly praise him for trying just a little. At some point Ganador will canter, you must believe me. Perhaps not perfectly, but canter he will …'*

Ganador refused to canter for one week, or five training sessions. On the first day of the second week his misunderstandings finally came to an end. Defiance was now his only weapon. I could see rebelliousness in every line of his body every flash of his eyes. By the second his behavior became more unpredictable, frenzied even. Ganador was totally opposed to any kind of forward going canter and showed his non co-operation by leaping, plunging and attempting to climb the boards of the school. He remembered the searing pain of his breaking, when studs dug into his nostrils, leaving not a scar, but the ornate design of nail heads upon his once velvety smooth nose. Then, without warning he cantered! Not one stride, but 'seven' forward bounds of the missing pace. After seven wonderful strides, he stopped dead, his eyes wild with fear. He threw his head up high; eyes staring upwards, away from his tormentors, unmoving and motionless he prepared himself for the pain that he remembered followed each and every stride of canter. High class carriage horses do not canter, they trot or passage and now he was learning rules from a different book.

Quickly Geoff dismounted. He stroked the stallion's neck and smiled his first really happy smile in three weeks.

I stood and clapped, Shelly cheered.

"Ganador cantered!" she said. "I always knew he would, never doubted the fact." Her grin was from ear to ear.

"What did it feel like Geoff?" I queried. "It must have come as a shock after Ganador's lengthy impasse."

"Well ... I suppose it felt like going to Mars." Geoff remembered the seven magical strides over and over again. "But it's going to take time," his reply sounded a note of caution. He understood the complex difficulties the stallion encountered only too well. Patterns of behavior became more deeply ingrained with a horse, especially when those habits were acquired at a young age. Retraining the older problem horse could be a lengthy, often hazardous business, with no guarantee of any permanent improvement.

"On the proviso, his good days outnumber his bad, I'm happy." ... At least for now I thought...

\*

The day following Ganador's first canter strides was agreed by all to be a holiday, a celebration day, a do what you please day.

"Time to relax," said Geoff, riding up to me on Donovan in that easy way of his. "Fancy a ride out?" So I rode Ganador. I felt so very happy ... Geoff didn't need to say anything; the shortened stirrup leathers said it all. This would be a wild ride, a ride to remember.

At the graveyard, we rode down a rarely used path which led out to the uninhabited spread of the middle moors.

"Let's go!" he shouted.

Ganador raised his powerful neck high, transferring his weight back onto his haunches. For a moment, I thought he was going to rear, and then he lifted off with a surge of power. And we galloped across the moors … There was only one way, only one track firm enough to race on. It was a track the width of two ponies or one horse and cart and perilously close to steaming bogs. To the left, it cut across the moors to Lancashire's pennine way, to the right, it led into Yorkshire's limestone country. Ganador chose the way. I left everything to him. He took the left track, the old escape route for highwaymen. I pictured stagecoaches driving over the moorland road in dense swirling mists, robbers lying in wait preparing to strike - and then flying over the moors without a backward glance, across this secret path - silent, like ghosts, away into the mist…

Although I'd often galloped across this path, I'd never gone so fast, never felt like this. My pulse raced. I felt terrified yet excited, both at the same time. Ganador's strides never lessened, he ran at his own speed, the speed of the wind. His strides were of the air. Now the only sounds were of flying hoof beats and the distant howling of a nearby storm. The wind blew hard in my face, through my hair, my eyes streamed, it took my breath away. Swirling mist turned to cold rain. But nothing mattered anymore, I was living a dream … Ganador was galloping as naturally as he breathed. At last he felt free.

When he finally slowed down we were heading towards a lake. Thin sunlight shone down through a break in the layers of clouds, the surface of the water sparkled like diamonds; damp grass shimmered silver. A sign read Mereclough … I'd ridden past the Lancashire boundary. Rolling pennine countryside stretched out before me, the fencing was of post and rails and it warned of privately owned land. After resting for a few minutes I turned Ganador back towards the moors. The trail climbed slowly away from any shimmering grass and crossed an outcropped area of semi moorland, where the landscape soon grew wild and unfarmed. I could see only endless acres of windswept moor on either side of the pathway.

At the place where the clouds seemed to drop lower and crumbling stone walls took the place of fenced enclosures, I found

Geoff. We rode in single file, towards the middle of the moors back across the secret track, the only sound, the blowing of horses and sighing of the wind.

As we neared the bogs the mist thickened, it was low and rippling, a wind howled in the distance. One by one, we passed the shadows of no man's land ... mysterious, unexplained. A hamlet lying in ruins surrounded by bogs, a place where no-one lived or trod its paths, no man and no animal.

Eventually, we entered dry stone wall country where hamlets such as ours floated in the dark grey mist of winter. There was nothing and no-one to disturb the horses, or so I thought ... But my dream ended when I heard footfalls treading the soggy undergrowth and a voice calling out of the fog ... the unmistakable voice of Carlton, he stood by a farm gate.

"Well now, what tha doing out here?" As he spoke, he shoved what looked to be a measuring stick under his coat.

"Fancy meeting Carlton by the bogs," said Geoff. "More to the point is what you are doing here."

"Sizing job up Lad, that's what I'm doing." When Carlton said 'sizing job up,' the matter was closed and no further information would be revealed. "But av got some news if tha interested."

"Is it important news?" I had to shout because Ganador walked steadily backwards, his way of showing displeasure about standing still when out on a ride.

"New neighbors Lass- if tha really wants t' know." I was very interested and lost no time in turning Ganador around and backing him down to the gate. If he preferred to walk backwards, then so be it.

"Oer yonder," he said. "That abandoned place." He pointed to a desolate farm, almost in ruins, a place that locals preferred not to visit because of its many treacherous bogs.

"But who would be stupid enough to live out there?"

Carlton lowered his voice before replying, "Londoner's," he said grimly. "Man wears his hair in a pony tail, and woman looks reet peculiar, long skirts an all."

"Londoner's probably thought same of you Carlton when you

emerged out of a mist cloud in trench coat and baling band- must have thought they'd seen a ghost lost on moors."

"It's those hippies who are lost on moors Geoff. I belong here. I'm Yorkshire bred and born and proud of it." Carlton glared at Geoff, after all Geoff was still an off comer.

Geoff didn't understand the ways of the moors - neither did he realize Yorkshire's moors were under threat, from an invading army of hippies.

"What tha growin Lad? I said, real friendly like. "Tha tekin a lot o plant pots in."

"Pretty green leaves Grandpa," he said all clever like. "It's very good stuff if you want any for your pipe"

"He tried to sound funny, but I weren't listenin to any bedtime stories."

"Av some more news too- Guess what Londoner's are callin place?"

"Mayfair..." I said, thinking of my last shopping trip to the capital.

"Tha wrong Lass- Kabul Farm!"

"But we already have a Baghdad cottage Carlton..."

"Aye, and that's another Londoner, selling Afghan coats and what av you on markets. This is bloody Yorkshire, not Kabul or Baghdad."

Suddenly, everything was beginning to fit into place. The Yorkshire moors of all places. Never in a million years would I have imagined that 'good stuff' was grown locally. Not until now that is.

"Silly billy asked me what kind o weather we got...."

"Its solid Yorkshire weather Lad, and sheep seem to like it."

Carlton half turned and then addressed himself to Geoff. "It's like this Lad," he paused for added drama and walked closer to Donovan. "They know what we're up to, but we don't know what they're up to. If tha compares a democracy t' old Iron Curtain, thall knows what I mean..." And Carlton disappeared in the mist, or the mist fell over Carlton. Quickly we went on our way in the covering of mist...

On detouring past the new neighbor's place, I noticed KABUL FARM had already been painted on its wooden gate. In the driveway, lay a plastic structure waiting to be fixed together.

When we arrived back home, I told Michelle all the exciting news about our new neighbors.

"Really Norma, people grow 'good stuff' everywhere nowadays. But surely it's too cold to grow anything out here?" Michelle was not interested in gossip, not one jot. "Are you putting Ganador out? I love to see him free."

In mid afternoon, before the dark hills of winter cast their gloomy shadows over the farm, Shelly would lead Ganador to his paddock. I pretended to find leading him difficult, so I could stand back and watch his Kingly figure dancing down to the gate, to his area of freedom...

With no man on his back, plus soft ground underfoot he was able to move as nature intended; as his ancestors had thousands of years before. Here he would almost fly, only his wings were missing. His paces were of the air, the soft earth revealing little imprint from his hooves.

On the day following those momentous first canter strides, history was made, as Ganador cantered in freedom on his paddock. I saw a proud gleam enter his eyes, as he paused for a moment beside the field gate where I stood together with Michelle. After throwing his head up high, he drew himself together before gracefully galloping down to the gorge.

After that wonderful day, slowly, over a period of weeks, Ganador became stronger. He trusted his rider a little more and defying all expectations, began to canter off from both left and right leads, not every day, but sometimes, just as Fernando had prophesied.

*"He is always listening to you,*
*He listens even to your thoughts,*
*For his desire is to serve his master"*

*N Jimenez*

# *Mid-Winter*...Yorkshire Moors
# ...1980

# 16. 'Douggie'

Each winter, the high moors of North Yorkshire were swept by blinding, drifting blizzards, and soon the first snow of winter would fall. Following winter storms, large, startling white snowflakes swirled round weightlessly before touching the ground. The landscape would be transformed from its mournful color of winter into a sparkling brilliant white.

Snow fell regularly throughout the months of midwinter, layer upon layer, forming drifts which sometimes towered above the farmhouse door.

Serious winter arrived suddenly and violently to Moonraker Heights. It arrived with Siberian temperatures, blizzards and thick snow. This was about to happen. I could feel it in the air, even prophecy that all this would come about.

Only Michelle held any doubts as to the implications of a serious winter but the uninitiated were always disbelieving. Geoff however, had become wise to the ways of the moor and this wisdom told him to search for a digging machine; preferably, with the addition of snow plough attachment. Geoff had suffered the back breaking toil of many moorland winters, and knew time was not on his side before the first blizzard of winter closed our access road, possibly for many weeks.

Fate played a part in finding a digging machine- fate in the form of Val. It was just before Val's lesson commenced when she spotted Geoff in the balcony, leafing through the pages of Farmer's Weekly.

"What are you looking for Geoff? If it's machinery, there's a farm center outside Mytholmroyd. I do believe the name is Douggie's." Geoff's eyes lit up on hearing this important information.

"Wonder if this Doug has any old, inexpensive digging machines, good enough to keep the snow from the door?" Doug was high in command at the local farmers club, he lived and breathed Yorkshire, loved the place, worshipped the rain even. Not even Carlton came up to his exacting dialect and knowledge of the area.

And it came to pass, that two hours later Geoff jumped into his land rover like a man possessed ready to follow Val to the land of diggers.

"Cheap digging machines do not hang about very long!" Geoff shouted out of the window, before disappearing up the track.

"I find it difficult to swallow all this talk of blizzards and snow drifts," Michelle paused and leaned on the broom, with a look of total disbelief. "If it does come about, then bang go my driving lessons which are block booked to begin next week." She stared blackly at the brush, before proceeding to vent her fury on sweeping the yard. For some reason, I felt guilty about snow interfering with Michelle's longed for driving lessons. After all I'd never warned her...

"You could rebook for later, or why not practice driving our land rover up and down the farm track? I'm sure Geoff would love to help you," I lied, using the 'l' word, knowing full well that Geoff hated all learner drivers, particularly lady learner drivers who he often said 'should learn to drive in special parks.'

Suddenly, there was the noise of a steam train gradually becoming closer "It's here!" she shouted, and turning into the yard there it was, Geoff's digging machine, incredibly noisy, extremely large and newly painted in vivid sunshine yellow. In the driver's seat sat a burly salt of the earth Yorkshire farmer. The machine lurched ponderously to the left after turning into the farm yard and quivered to a halt with a massive shudder. Turning off the engine, the man climbed down the tiny ladder, surveyed the scene and proceeded to walk over to Michelle. All stranger's spoke to her first; she had that certain look that spells authority.

"Real beauty she is-" he said appreciatively. "Works all day lass and never complains. If tha teks it steady lass, thal be reet."

Presumably, this Douggie considered Michelle to be a female digging machine operator. I laughed, but she looked insulted.

"His Sunday names Douglas lass, but most folk call him Douggie the digger," he proudly pointed to the lettering on the side of the door. "And I'm Doug," he announced dramatically, "better known as Douggie the digger man."

Drama was the spice of life to all who existed on the moor, after all nothing much ever happened except the weather, lambing and digging. We walked over to Douggie; carefully inspecting him for any signs of beauty.

"The only exquisite thing I can see is the shovel attachment," I whispered. "Just imagine not lifting a finger when the snow comes."

"There is something cute though," mused Shelly. "I think it must be his size, he has that gentle giant look."

Doug carried on instructing Geoff on which leaver lifted, dug or shoved. Geoff was grinning like a kid with a new toy as he practiced lifting and lowering the various shovels.

"This driver's seat is really comfortable. I could sit here all day!" he sounded thrilled, blissful even. "Come up and get the feel of it," he yelled down to me from his swivel seat.

"Tha' looks cappin up there Lad!" Doug bellowed up to Geoff. "Get thee up ladder Lass! Time waits for no man, or woman come to that! Thas' a fear of height Lass?" he asked chuckling.

"No way," I hissed, "the things almost tipping over. Anyway climbing that ladder counts me out."

The old digger possessed a medium to serious tremble, after all Douggie was all of twenty years old. I imagined anything would shake after twenty years of hard labor.

"Does it always shake so violently?" Michelle looked Doug straight in the eyes. This was her interrogation technique, perfected when working as a secretary for a solicitor. She claimed the stare never failed in revealing the truth.

"Always shakes lass, its nowt much, probably valve in combustion chamber. Still going strong he is, no sign of blood pressure yet. Douggie will see thee out lass!" Upon seeing her discomfort the digger man roared with laughter.

"Thav only a bit o' work lass," he looked round our normal sized farm yard, glancing at the lane. "This Lad's up to all exertion tha' can give him!" Michelle blushed and came to stand with me.

At this point, I thought it best to remain silent, not having the faintest idea on the importance of any mechanical part. The digger man and Geoff could have been speaking another language- a language that included mystery words such as combustion chamber. Geoff seemed to thrive on this other language and agreed that the machine would still be in use when we were finished.

"May I ask a question?" By now, Michelle wore a puzzled expression. "Does living on the Yorkshire moors considerably reduce the average life span? Because if 'he' outlives me, I will definitely have to find a more sheltered place to park my bones. I have more than fifty years to go before popping my clogs." She looked to have that sinking feeling, the one brought about by little knowledge of a subject. But then neither of us knew or pretended to know anything about the longevity of digging machines...

He patted the machine once again before counting out Geoff's money, and then squeezed it into his already bulging wallet.

"Thall be thankful tha' bought Douggie. Do all tha' work, all thav got to give it lad, I tell thee no lie." Doug and Geoff laughed heartily before continuing their conversation on the miracle of engines. Climbing into Geoff's land rover they swiftly departed back to the paradise for digging machines, which lay somewhere beyond Mytholmroyd Village ... or in Doug's words, my home by the river...

# 17 Trapped in a blizzard

*December 10*

On the day following Douggie's adoption the sky shone a brilliant blue, any threat of imminent snow seeming to have disappeared overnight. It was just the kind of day to enjoy a trek over the moors ... I saddled Ganador up and Geoff Donovan who would lead.

"This is Ganador's first long ride." I felt so happy, everything was coming together at last. "How about riding over to Hardcastle Crags?"

"It's a long way, over half a day there and back?"

"But it's my favorite place ... please?"

"You ought to stay close to home in winter, you never know." He swung round in the saddle and saw my forlorn face. "Come on then if we are going..."

The morning was like any other perfect winter morning except for a freezing cold wind which caused us to wear two of almost everything. After clearing the open moors we rode on narrow winding cart tracks before arriving at the entry into 'crag valley.' A spectacular forest; set in a deep gorge. One of nature's wonders - formed during the ice age, when glaciers had swept over the land, knocking it about and leaving a paradise for walkers or rock climbers. A place where all varieties of trees grew in abundance and crystal clear streams cascaded down to the river in the base of the gorge. As we began the descent to the floor of the valley, robins hopped from branch to branch seeming to play with the horses, following them down to the woods by the river. In the distance, I heard the song of a blackbird. A small number of song birds often nested in the lowest woodlands of the gorge, throughout the winter. We rode from beginning to end of the woodlands and then along the river bank towards the spot where river, streams, and waterfalls all merged into one. Unexpectedly, the sky darkened with the blackness of night, low dark clouds blotting out the light of day. The birds stopped singing, and all around there was a heavy stillness as the forest waited…

"Oncoming blizzard, let's get out-" Geoff shouted. His voice echoed in the silence of the valley, it seemed to spring left, then right, until fading away completely.

"Can we not stay here?"

"Fills up with snow–we'd freeze to death, got to get back."

"But I feel faint…I want to stop? Just can't stop shivering."

"Keep moving, swing your arms about, quit the stirrups, move your legs."

Although I didn't realize it, the deadly beginnings of hypothermia were reaching out towards me. The core temperature of my body was dropping below normal, circulation was slowing down. Even though I had seen and heard about it so many times before, this was different, what I'd seen had no connection to me – but it never has when it's you. The movement helped a little, but my energy was soon gone, it just floated away.

"Let's turn through the forest now … you take the lead." So we turned the horses towards home with Ganador leading the way. As we climbed higher the howling wind grew deafening. A sleet storm crossed the fringes of the forest, and the footpath turned wet and slippery. The horses tried their hardest to climb the steep pathways, but Donovan often lost his footing - shale and stones fell away from the edge, hurtling down to the floor of the river. Just as I thought things couldn't get any worse, there was a noise like low thunder, but not from above from below … A strange rumbling sound.

"The paths going…"

"What should we do?"

"Get to the firm side–quick!" Then all I could hear was Geoff shouting "Forward… Move damn it…" but it was too late, a piece of pathway had given way beneath Donovan. Wet earth and stones clattered down the face of the gorge, crashing into the river. Donovan stood totally still, his eyes wide with fear, his hind legs slipping on the wet earth. Geoff untied the coil of rope he always carried when riding out, the same rope I'd laughed at before setting out.

"Yorkshire's not the wild west Geoff," I'd said, ever so flippantly.

"Horses get sucked into bogs out there. It's called staying out of harm's way."

But I wasn't laughing now. He slung the rope round the base of a nearby tree, before he attached it to Donovan - it went in front of the saddle like a sling, round his neck and then between his forelegs. I watched horrified as soil trickled down the bank.

"Paths crumbling away..." I tried to shout but my voice didn't obey. Taking up the slack of the rope he walked over to Ganador and fixed it to him in exactly the same place.

"But Ganador could be pulled over the edge-" I screamed. "You can't do this." By now my hands and feet felt dead, time had no meaning. Each second seemed an eternity, like watching a film in slow motion, every movement slow and excruciatingly painful.

"You will have to get off. I want you to walk him forwards slowly, a step at a time. Please try..." Ganador pulled, and the rope tightened, he stretched his neck down, his nose touching the leaves on the footpath, all his power in his shoulders. I could swear he understands it's all up to him. Donovan fought for his life, flexing his legs high under his belly. In one last desperate attempt, he kicked out to find a foothold. I heard a sharp clang as a metal shoe found the hard rock side. It was then he did something remarkable, he rounded his back and jumped, he seemed to defy gravity. In an instant Donovan stood on the firm part of the pathway, as if nothing had happened. He rested a hind leg but he was safe.

Geoff brushed the soil from the saddle, rewound the rope, helped me into the saddle and then mounted.

"Better be moving..."

"What if he's lame?" I found it difficult to say the words, they sounded slurred.

"We have to get back - lame or not."

"I want to stay here ..." Nothing mattered anymore, only the desperate need to give in. Not living, not dying, just sleep. Any rational judgment had gone.

"Try to fight, we have to carry on."

"I'm past fighting…"

"It's the cold. Start counting from one to ten, forwards and backwards."

"One - two - three ..." I couldn't find four, any sense of realism had departed - I'd entered some kind of 'in between world', a void, which was neither conscious nor unconscious. Geoff must have ridden alongside, his voice screaming, just like the wind.

"Drop the reins ... Leave it to him."


When we left the trees behind, the wind raced across the moors, with such force it took my breath away. The low dark clouds move like a flood across the open country and it was then we met the eye of the blizzard ... It surrounded us with a terrible violence. Screaming winds lashed the freezing snow horizontally, but the horses refused to give way. I saw the shelter of a nearby wall. I desperately wanted its refuge. But Ganador shut my orders out. He made the decisions. And I was past fighting. Now, I can't hold the saddle pommel anymore, my hands have cramped up.

"Please let me shelter behind that wall…"

"You'd be dead in twenty minutes. Have to keep going." Fortunately Ganador met the blizzard head on, moving forwards into the storm, his ears stapled back.

"Try to hold the saddle. Start counting again" This time I counted to five before my head began to nod. Strangely the pain caused by the biting cold had gone - I felt exhausted and dizzy but I'd stopped shivering.

I remember Geoff fighting to be heard above the howling of the gale. He must be trying to wake me up. I felt an overpowering exhaustion, a need to collapse, to lie down behind anything that would stop the wind ...

"Think of the dead sheep, think of the hikers, frozen behind stone walls because they roamed the moors on the wrong day." Now I felt the same fatigue as the frozen hikers... I looked into the face of fate.

Somehow the horses found their way over the moor, moving as best they could through a thick wall of driving snow and swirling fog in that first blizzard of winter.

Two hours later we arrived home numb with cold and frozen by the driving snow. Michelle had cooked oat gruel to give warmth to the horses; she waited in the stables with a pile of warm towels from the house. I remember her voice asking 'what's wrong Norma?' Geoff helped me down the path into the farm. I felt crippled by the severe cold and found walking difficult. My fingers refused to unclench from their imaginary grip on the reins, until some hours later when wrapped in blankets in front of a log fire. Then, I at last gave way to sleep. Geoff turned the sofa into a warm bed where I rested for two days before my energy returned.

Following the blizzard snow fell softly for two days. At noon on the third day the snow stopped and the sky returned to a brilliant blue. This was a time when the rest of the world ceased to exist. When roads and pathways lay hidden under drifting snow and a hushed stillness filled the air.

Thick, dazzling white snow now covered the moors, which only three days before had been the color of dull grey. In the meadow soft murmurs from the stream became sharp and distinct. The bramble and gorse could be heard to part and crack beneath my feet, the river flowing through the gorge roared like an angry sea. Shelly said she could hear the cries of children playing, as far away as Todmorden.

After darkness fell and night lights glowed, long thick icicles blinked and twinkled in the stable yard. Each icicle perfectly crafted and a masterpiece of beauty. Shelly named them 'hanging jewels,' our very own collection of ice art – glittering like a passageway straight from a fairy tale, within the farm yard. After the horses were fed and rugged up warmly for the freezing nights, we stayed down in the stables wrapped in horse blankets, watching icicles sparkling under the light of the moon and listening to Christmas music.

"After all … can't miss one minute of a special time like this, can we now. We may never see such a sight ever again, unless we visit the North Pole."

Exactly one week later the magnificent icicles and dazzling snow began to melt slowly away. For some uncertain reason the warmth of the sun became similar to that of the towns in the valley, where blizzards never raged and screaming winds were only to be imagined. The pure new snow changed from featherlike, to slush - a soiled reminder of our winter wonderland. For a short time the freezing cold of the high places had abandoned the moor, and we shivered in the same damp chilly cold of the mill towns far below. A thin dancing mist shrouded the hills with a veil of the palest grey, always a sign of future rain. Tomorrow the moorland road which led to the towns would be passable, it would be safe to drive to the airport and collect Mum. In my mind, I planned a perfect Christmas dinner and imagined where a second tree could stand. But then I remembered the blizzard and wondered when the next snow would fall.

"Will it be a white Christmas Geoff?"

"Hope not, we can't have Mum stranded at the airport."

"Don't tell her about the blizzard? She would only worry."

"What blizzard?"

"I feel so excited!"

"Your nothing but a dreamer–do you know that?"

"Course I know … but the world needs dreamers. This year, I'm buying two sets of fairy lights, one for the tree, and a set for the stable yard, as similar to icicles as possible."

"Come on, back to earth, and help me sweep the yard again, the drains can't cope with all this water."

'For through his mane and tail the high wind sings.
Fanning the hairs what wave like feathered wings.

William Shakespeare.

# 18. Christmas and Mum

*December 21. – January 1. 1981!*

Mum arrived five days before Christmas, just when the icicles had almost dripped away. There was still plenty of snow to be seen, especially on the highest hills, but the severe cold had gone ... at least for now. She flew into Manchester airport where I anxiously waited outside arrivals.

"Here I am!" she said "I can see you at last. You will never know how concerned I've been." If only I'd pulled myself together at Dads funeral, thought of her, buried my own grief... I could have spared her the worry. An emotional daughter was the last thing she needed.

"Now it's my turn to worry," I said. "Are you warm enough for outside? Because it's cold, blustery, and sopping wet..."

"Can't wait to get to the farm, I've imagined this moment for such a long time." It was thrilling to hear her voice again, far better than any Christmas present. On making our way to the car park, she began to shiver uncontrollably. "Do you know," she said faintly, "I felt like collapsing as soon as that bitter wind hit me. I don't know how you stand this freezing cold. The weather's warm and sunny in Seville"

"You get used to anything in time Mum."

"I do hope so..."

"Geoff's turned the central heating up. Promise you'll be warm at home."

"Thank goodness for that."

"By the way Mum, Billy rang this morning- he wants to take us out shopping before Christmas"

"I'll ring him tonight and organize a time then..."

On the following day, as soon as Mum saw the untidy state of the farm kitchen, she set to work to create an appearance of order. Very quickly everything shone like new, and unfilled spaces appeared on the work top, in places I never knew existed.

On the day before Christmas Eve, Billy drove up to the farm. He took Mum and me to Manchester, where the traffic was dreadful. Everyone with a car, living in the county of Lancashire must have thought the same thing... 'Let's buy the presents in Manchester,' for the roads were packed. Mum had to buy her Christmas presents on Oxford street as not one parking space could be found anywhere near the city center.

"I think Manchester was a good choice for shopping," exclaimed Billy, as he loaded Mums presents into the boot. There followed an uncomfortable silence before she spoke. "To be truthful Billy, I much prefer to shop in Hebden Bridge, its smaller and more personnel, a place where people still speak to each other. You can laugh, but it's true." Billy was not laughing, his face had turned an unhealthy shade of purple, he was furious.

"I'm not laughing Mum," he said convincingly. "Why didn't you tell me all this before we set off? I've been driving for six long hours."

"Calm down Billy..." Mum said sternly. "It's Christmas!"

When we arrived home, I was surprised to find that Michelle had prepared dinner. She'd cooked a delicious Spaghetti Bolognaise, served with olives, tomatoes and courgettes.

"It's a recipe out of 'You are what you eat,' full of vitamins and olive oil, just what you need in winter." She loved having Mum over and followed her about like a lap dog, making frequent and plentiful quantities of tea and piling numerous supplies of cushions next to every chair.

"What do you miss the most when you come to the farm?" Shelly asked Mum over dinner.

"Firstly the lovely weather, secondly flamenco - it's my passion.

And after that, the more relaxed life style over there…. But I adore being here at the farm. Dad and I planned to retire here one day, decorate a small cottage and do some walking. That's all gone now, it's just a memory."

"Flamenco's not very popular in England," replied Shelly. "It may be due to the cold weather; I think passionate music like flamenco requires hot blooded people."

"How right you are dear," said Mum.

"Seeing we're in Yorkshire and not Seville…who fancies a walk to the Shepherd?" asked Geoff. "There's clog dancing in the barn tonight … And what's so funny?"

"What a good idea Geoff," said Mum. "I've never seen anyone dancing with clogs on before. Let's all go up to the pub and let me buy the drinks- just give me ten minutes to make myself look presentable."

After dinner, Billy went into the sitting room. Billy was an information addict, he checked out four newspapers a day, morning radio and evening television, always news channels. He said that any single source of information could never be trusted and he was probably right.

"Come and sit here Sis," he moved a pile of cushions out of the way and patted the adjoining seat. "Not had a proper talk for months."

"Did you take the trip to Portugal Billy?" I knew that special arrangements had been made … His role was to see the state of play, list the arms he saw about, the make, type, availability.

"Blooming nightmare Sis," he said teasing. "Ian fell in the sea and Ed needed treatment for a dirty mosquito bite."

"Not on the beach … What did you see?"

"There was a tank on the same road as the hotel. You should have seen the holiday maker's faces!"

"Not in use I hope?"

"Oh no, children were playing in it, but tanks put the fear of God into people."

"What's it all been about? It felt like a threatening thunder storm, one which never really happened."

"A little Moscow in Iberia ... and the world's in their hands, links to France, then through the rest of Europe."

"Why not south into North Africa ..."

"Europe's important strategically, nobody wants North Africa Sis, too much trouble, been given the thumbs down. Religion waves the flag over there ... The Arab states will fall apart soon enough, and nobody wants to be there when they do."

"How long can it go on for?"

"How longs a piece of string? If you keep chipping away Sis, you arrive at a point of weakness. And until Spain and Portugal get their respective acts together ... the Commis' will keep knocking on their doors. You see, times not an issue, they play the waiting game. Anyway, Mum tells me you were over there?"

"I visited Santarem, a town in the Ribatejo. Went over to see Golega Fair, it was fascinating." I didn't dare tell him about meeting a mercenary, maybe Rimo was on the wanted list. Who knows? Mum walked into the room at that instant, I felt so relieved. Billy had a way of controlling conversations, finding out secrets, things I did not want to say.

"Are we ready then?"

"We've been ready for the past half hour Mum," Billy always took the bait. "Let's use my car, far too cold for walking; anyway I have to drive home after. Let old Geoff enjoy a drink or two!"

*

One by one, we felt our way into the dimly lit bar, only to hear the voice of Carlton telling his farmer friends about his most recent 'get rich quick' brainwave. We sat by the fire and listened.

"And its nowt to do with subsidy forms..." Carlton saluted the bar man, like he always did when ordering his first pint of the night, and then he slowly lit his pipe.

"Come on Carlton, get on with it Lad."

"Thall have to wait tha time Herbert- this is important." Only when beer and pipe were to his satisfaction did he continue "Blizzards and snow are sent for a purpose Lads and that's to make

164

money." His disciples hung onto his every word, the bar was in total silence and any chatter had faded away. Everyone wanted to know how to make extra cash. "If tha daft enough to drive up t' moors in unfavorable conditions … Tha daft enough to pay me hundred quid for towing thee back on road."

"Carlton's right-towing out costs money. We offer a service," Zak said weakly. "What does Vet think?"

"I always thought," David scratched his head and swung round to face his audience, "that towing a fellow motorist out of danger is doing a good turn?" David lacked the bite of a true Yorkshire man … his education got in the way; five years at Oxford had softened him. The Yorkshire grit he once possessed had gone away.

"Thav got it wrong David Lad," said Carlton. "Would thee drive a car up t' moors in a blizzard? Thav got more sense."

"I damn well have to sometimes, and in the middle of the night … I get called out to help you farmers."

"And what do you think Evelyn?" Carlton left his stool to greet Mum, "You look a picture Lass…" He kissed her; I'd never seen Mum blush red before, but she did after Carlton's welcome. Fortunately, she knew enough about the ways of the moor, to know she must find a simple solution. Tonight was not the time to offend anyone, whatever she thought, for tomorrow was Christmas Eve.

"I think warning signs should be placed at the bottom of the Steeps, after all, how does a driver know there's a blanket of snow on the moors? And what happens if people don't have one hundred pounds in their car?"

"Norma's Mum has a point there." Zachariah's words just tumbled out, and for a moment there was an uncomfortable silence before Carlton answered.

"Them that can't or won't pay get left in snow for next lad who comes along."

"That's not very nice is it Carlton?"

"Life's not nice Evelyn, but we grin and bear it up here."

"How about coming over to Seville for a holiday?" asked Mum, changing the subject, "why not get away from the moors and the cold? I'm sure you could do with a break."

"Do you know Lass - I'd be over like a shot if I didn't have a farm to look after."

"Thav got two farms now Lad... Not one..." Zachariah spoke without thinking. He'd just told everyone Carlton's biggest secret– the news about his clandestine purchase of a second farm.

There was total silence now, everyone wanted to know more on the subject of Carlton's second farm. Bert behind bar, folded his cloth neatly and placed it over the pumps, no beer would be pulled tonight until he'd heard every word.

"Does your Mother like the new farm?" Mum had a way of planting revealing questions; she should have worked as a prosecutor, or so Geoff thought.

"Never would you find my old Mother living in middle o moors Evelyn. She likes village too much. Break her heart if she moved away from Heptonstall; finish her off good and proper it would."

"I think I know what you're planning," said Mum. "It's a bachelor pad. I'm right aren't I?" Mum would continue chipping away until she had him cornered.

"Now it's not what mother would call livable in, not yet, and mores the pity. Anyway, there's a tenant in, so place is kept warm."

"So you bought the farm as an investment? Or did you buy it for its grazing?" And Carlton fell straight into her trap.

"I bought it because there's moorland grazing rights on deeds and not many places can boast o that."

"It must feel like owning the moors..." Mum said sweetly.

"That it does!"

"You always were a business man Carlton." There she goes I thought, telling him what he wants to hear, making him feel good.

"I've always done my best Evelyn."

"I know you have Carlton," said Mum kindly.

"What's this 'ere farm called?" Bert behind bar straightened up from his crouched position over the pumps.

"I'm calling it Willy Fox Farm." The minute he said Willy's name, everything fit into place. Everyone smiled and cheered and the hum of conversation returned.

"Tribute to Willy Fox Lads," called Bert. "Drinks on house..."

And when all the free drinks had been drunk, the farmer's took off their caps and bought more, saying that 'no better man ever set foot on Yorkshire's moors.' Bert picked up his cloth and began pulling pints. Carlton's second home with grazing rights would now have top billing over Christmas…and well into the New Year.

"Here," said Carlton. He pushed a large hanky into Mums hand. "Can't abide a woman's tears, never could. What tha crying for Lass?"

"It's the atmosphere Carlton, there's nothing like this in Spain," sniffled Mum.

"Tha needing a change Lass, that's all. Yorkshire's full o warm friendly folk, tha can feel safe in Yorkshire. Spain's for holiday's not living. Are you and family staying to see entertainment?"

"We are Carlton. Is clog dancing a local dance?"

"Started in cotton mills - workers used to step together, or so they say."

The entertainment was held in the Shepherd's barn, the extra lighting came in the form of one extra string of fairy lights placed on the few remaining branches of a plastic tree. The four Cloggers were dressed in top hats, gaiters, long socks with bells below the knee, and the all important footwear, clogs. When the men jumped up and down the noise was overwhelming. It reminded me of Morris dancing, except for the clogs, top hats, and nerve shattering din.

"I like the jingling bells," Mum said gamely, "reminds me of the driving horses in Jerez."

"Well I've had enough Lass, bells or no bloody bells." We followed Carlton out of the barn, and down the passageway which led to the covered oak door, the entry to the bar.

"I hope tha floors well insured Herbert, with them twerps jumping about thall need it." And Carlton ordered his last pint of the night. "Home and horizontal before midnight, as mother always says. Goodnight and God bless. I'm looking forward to seeing you again Evelyn. Don't forget Lass…"

"Goodnight Carlton, I won't forget."

Before Billy left for home he asked me a strange question.

"Just tell me the truth Sis - I've no idea what this place is about, or what those guys in fancy dress are up to. Have you?"

"You mean the local farmers Billy? They all wear baling band accessories, nothing strange about that."

"Sound more like con men to me Sis, if you know what I'm saying." I saw Mum coming over to say goodbye, so I nodded my head … Anyway, how could Billy possibly understand the ways of the moor? Places like the Shepherd didn't exist. Neither did characters resembling the local farmers.

"Lovely night out wasn't it Billy?"

"It was certainly a night with a difference Mum…"

\*

The freezing weather returned on Christmas Eve, valley and meadow shone a sparkling white, covered in crisp new frost. The distant hills were only visible through a delicate veil of silver mist, setting a limit to our visual world. After breakfast, Mum sliced carrots for the horses in readiness for the morning walk down to the stables.

"I'd love to see Ganador drink his morning tea. I can't believe he can sip from a cup." After wrapping up well, we filled the stove with logs and ventured out into the cold. Mum carrying the cup of tea.

"I'm cleaning his box out for Christmas," said Shelly. "Ganador's out on his paddock."

At that second, I heard the hue and cry of scream's and galloping hoof beats on the frozen earth, and then I saw a hiker come flying over the style, the one adjoining Ganador's paddock. Oh dear I thought, footpaths and walkers rights equal trouble, a bed of nails in fact. I'd spent a fortune on fencing the footpath with sturdy posts and rails, so it was separated from Ganador's paddock.

Then I saw Ganador, he sailed over the five barred gate with only one thought in his mind - the hiker. For reasons I never understood, the sight of a back pack or Tyrolean hat returned the horse to his earlier life with the Gypsies. Running across the track, the man took refuge in a corner of the stable yard, closely followed by Ganador. The stallion was playing the role he knew so well, that of a guard horse, the one he remembered from the scrap yard. As calmly as possible, I walked over to the horse, held my hand up to his awesome head and said, "Away." Spinning round the stallion trotted over to the gate, jumped back into the paddock, dropped his head to the ground and pretended to graze. I stared at the man, who was still shouting, and my heart sank when I saw his face. He was chairman of hiker's rights, a land owner's nightmare. A strange man, who loved making trouble, often left gates open, even complained about mud on footpaths. All in all, he was a man I did not trust. In her usual charming way Mum saved the situation from becoming worse. She came walking round the corner carrying Ganador's cup of tea and waved her magic wand over the irate hiker.

"I think you need this cup of tea young man, you have certainly earned it." The sight of Mum walking towards him with a cup of tea stopped him shouting straight away - I even thought I saw a flicker of a smile.

"Look what he's wearing Norma," Shelly said scathingly, "he'd scare the daylight's out of man or beast." He wore a Tyrolean hat embellished with a peacock feather. Before walking away, he turned and looked towards me. I was sure he shouted 'Happy Christmas...'

# 19. The Eve of Christmas

*Toby Jug Farm, Christmas Eve*

On the Eve of Christmas, Mum and I wrapped presents whilst listening to Verdi's Requiem, something we always did at Christmas.

"Can I open mine now?" she asked. "I know it's naughty but I don't believe in Santa Claus."

"Why not - saves the wrapping paper."

She slowly read the name out on the cover, "Concerto de Aranjuez, for guitar and orchestra, by a Spanish composer, and of the classical school... how unusual."

"Put it on, see if you like it." The opening bars of the Allegro cast its spell and we stopped wrapping presents, they could wait till later, but this moment was special. Mum read the performance instructions out:

'It is meant to sound like the hidden breeze, that stirs the tree tops in the park ... It should be as strong as a butterfly and as dainty as a veronica'

"What beautiful words," she said, "and what lovely music. The soloist's cadenzas are technically brilliant, especially against the sweep of the strings."

"We played this concerto at the Christmas Concert, and I never knew a Spanish guitar could sound so overwhelming, but it did. In the Adagio tears rolled down my cheeks, it was very emotional. At one time, the entire orchestra had to stop ... fortunately it happened at the get together, before the evening concert. The conductor threatened to cancel the performance, if there were any more tears."

"Did his threat work?"

"Not completely, how can mere words prevent emotion?" Each time I thought of that performance, I remembered how uptight the string section had been, concentrating on keeping tears away and missing cues twice. Fortunately, the audience never noticed the bungled entries; they just heard the beauty of the music and the effortless mastery of the soloist. "Since then, I've played and listened to the Adagio countless times ... but the music still brings tears to my eyes."

"It never harms to cry, you've spoiled me..."

I awoke to the sounds of snowflakes softly touching the window panes, clinging together in crystals until only one tiny peep hole remained. Geoff was already out digging a pathway down to the stables. I could hear his shovel and Michelle's voice. After dressing in two of everything, I walked over to the six tiny mullioned windows and wiped away a patch of steam. The view was incredible ... it felt unreal, just like the Inn and the farmers. Delicate chiffon mist obscured the distant hills, and a sea of clouds rested over the valley. The summits climbed out of the mist, their tops startling white with snow ... just hanging in the air like magic. It must have snowed in the night, as I slept, or when Mum and I wrapped presents, listening to the requiem, or the concerto, listening to beautiful music behind closed curtains and meter thick walls.

Suddenly I felt a surge of guilt; I'd forgotten to check outside last night, forgotten to listen for the howl of an oncoming storm - something I always did in winter. The normal signs of snowstorms, stillness and darkness went unnoticed at night, listening was the only way.

"A blizzard swept in, around two a.m." Geoff told us over breakfast. "Did no one hear me battling down to the stables? It's not a serious one as blizzards go, but the top doors were open. Almost forgot what day it is ... Happy Christmas everyone!" So Geoff had gone down to close the stable doors, in the middle of the night. Any box facing into the wind during a snow storm could mean hypothermia for the trapped animal, freezing, possibly to death...

"Never heard a whisper Geoff," sleeping through a blizzard made me feel responsible of a crime.

"Sorry Geoff..." said Shelly. "I never heard a storm, didn't wake up once."

"I'm not complaining-" said Mum contentedly. "This never happens in Seville!" she sighed happily, completely oblivious of the near tragedy. "A white Christmas trapped on the moors, how exciting. Shall we open the presents now, and then relax over coffee?" Thank goodness Mum had no idea what all the fuss was about. "Just look at that view, it's exactly like a painting."

"Carlton will be pleased," Geoff said drily as he handed the presents out. "He's probably counting the extra cash already."

"It's as well some ones there to pull cars out, even if he does charge. What do you think Michelle?"

"I think you're right."

"If I have dinner ready for mid-afternoon... am I allowed a request Geoff? More than anything in this world, I'd love to see you riding Ganador." She paused before continuing. "You see, I've been rather naughty, because the other night I invited Carlton and Zachariah to come round for a Christmas drink at about one. I thought we could all watch my Ganador being put through his paces..."

Before the riding commenced, we ate warm mince pies and sipped Jerez sherry.

"Delicious Evelyn, I can taste the sun."

"I think you would like Jerez Carlton, it's surrounded by grape farms ... the homeland of sherry."

By this time, Geoff had put saddle and bridle on Ganador, so we all trooped into the yard to watch him mount. The minute Geoff's toe touched the stirrup iron, the stallion wanted to be off, the sound of his iron shoes on stone cobbles was reminiscent of thunder.

"Does Geoff want him to do that Norma? It looks terribly dangerous," said Mum. "I have never seen a horse with so much energy; he's looking for the next battle."

Once inside the school Ganador charmed everyone, performing

difficult movements effortlessly, displaying his abilities and showing off his master. The object of today was allowing the stallion to be himself ... and to forget all about correct training. Today was special.

"There's never been anything to compare with this Lad tha knows," Carlton sipped yet another glass of 'sunshine,' "he's what you'd call ... unique."

"It's a privilege just to watch the Lad." Zak had brought a little present, six bottles of Yorkshire beer for Ganador, "Extra strong-" he said. "Put one in mash tonight Geoff, do him a world o good, help him feel warmer it will."

And a happy Christmas was had by all...

# 20. Moorland Rave Up

*Diary, New Years Eve*

*'Christmas week has passed without a hitch, it's just as it should be ... peaceful and quiet. Yesterday, Mum met up with some of her old friends, had dinner with Val at Graham's new restaurant in the next valley and sailed down the canal in a barge towed by a nineteen hands high Shire horse... he was enormous. Tonight is New Years Eve, Mother's last night at the farm, tomorrow she flies to Seville, and I will miss her terribly...'*

"Well," she said finally. "That's another one gone." As Mum said 'gone' she threw her 1980 diary into the litter bin. "A terrible year, perhaps next year will be better. I'm off upstairs to pack now, always keeping my fingers crossed of course."

"What about Mum?"

"I must be worrying about blizzards in the night. I can't wait to get back to Seville and home."

"When you say 'back home' it hurts, I do wish you lived here."

"Maybe one day I will..."

At three a.m. something woke me up, I didn't know what it was, I felt so tired ... The only thing I remember is looking at the clock and feeling irritated, but not knowing why. Closing my eyes I tried to relax, but darkness didn't arrive. I opened them, and gazed at flashing lights on the long bedroom wall, the one across from the four poster bed. Just to make sure I was awake and not dreaming I pinched myself. The wall glowed with moving colored lights, just watching the bedroom illumination caused me to feel dizzy, it had to be strobe lighting…but from what source? I hated flashing lights. Jumping out of bed, I walked over to the window and to my surprise there were lights dancing over the valley and meadow. They moved in circles, figure of eights, or straight up into the sky, it was a scene from a West End musical … or had the Northern Lights relocated to the Yorkshire moors?

"Wake up Geoff," I hissed in his ear. Geoff would know the answer, he was practical.

"I can't," he said narkily. "I need to sleep…go away."

Eventually, he came over to the windows and threw one open. The cold was intense and biting. The fields were sparkling white with a covering of snow and frost.

"Looks as if a refugee camps set up in the next field," he walked over to the drawers to find his new binoculars, "come and look." Geoff sounded totally unruffled. How could he feel unconcerned when a refugee camp had sprung up in the next field, and in the middle of the night?

At least twenty white tents now stood on the other side of my stone wall, on the field belonging to the Inn, a quiet meadow used only for making hay. And then the noise began… mad, crazy, rap. I felt shaken to the core; the moors were silent, except for the wind.

"Is it a pop festival?"

"Doubt it," he said wearily. "This is top of the moors on December thirty first with a minus fifteen temperature outside. I'm going out to see what the hell's going on." As Geoff's temper flared, so the rap grew louder and faster. "Speakers must be all round the field…" and off he stomped, throwing his outdoor clothes on as he went.

All the commotion had disturbed mother, now she was knocking on the bedroom wall. Surely she didn't think I of all people would be listening to earsplitting rap in the middle of the night. After waiting for what seemed a long minute, I did exactly the same as Geoff. Throwing on my warmest clothes I followed in his footsteps down the stairs and across the farmyard. The first thing that hit me were dazzling lights, the field had been lit up like a motor way – but not with cars, instead, there were hundreds of leather clad bodies dancing and drinking around a bonfire, or rolling on the frost covered ground.

"Stay down and keep quiet," ordered Geoff. Tiptoeing over to the footpath we peeped over the wall. "It's the new neighbors from Kabul farm, the people Carlton's going mad about," Geoff whispered.

I could see all the way into a brightly lit tent which stood beyond our wall. The tent was set out like a flower shop, but selling only one plant. There were hundreds of plastic flower pots, all filled with pretty green leaves - some with tiny blue flowers. At the opposite side of the wall was a queue, with every single face looking eager to purchase at least one pot of green leaves. So Carlton had been correct...

"Celebrate the New Year man!" said a voice from the other side of the wall.

"Peace and goodwill man!" another voice added, there was a definite look of Javier to the owner of the second voice.

Unknown to me, Mother had ventured into the yard ... she stood in slippers, dressing gown and wooly hat and held a torch.

"There's a land rover behind the tent," she hissed from her position on the mounting block. "It's full of plant pots and white toffee bags." Mum seemed to be enjoying the drama. "London twangs except for one unmistakable foreign accent. Now what on earth are they doing up here?"

"I don't know Mum I feel too cold to care."

"And so do I. Shall we leave them to it?" Back we crept into the warmth of the farm. "Whatever next?" she said frowning. "Does it not worry you Norma that hippies and foreigners are camping out on your doorstep?"

"The man with the foreign accent wore an Indian headband," added Geoff for good measure.

"I'm making three hot toddies," she said. "We almost froze to death out there. Nothing like a hot toddy for restoring the circulation..."

Dawn broke with the noise of short regular knocks on the farm door. "It's the police," I guessed, "I know the sound." Geoff answered the door.

"Happy New Year to you all," the officer said without smiling. "Were you out last night in your car Sir?"

"No, I was in all night."

"Have you anyone to vouch for that?" a plain clothes man said.

"Yes I have-"

"Before we depart, I need to examine your car Sir. It's the same make and color as reported by a witness."

"Follow me Officer," Geoff sounded tired, frustrated and shocked all in one. He threw on coat and boots and walked down to his garage, to the converted cow shed where his elderly white e type resided. The policemen scraped mud from tyres and dust from seats, which they put into plastic bags. As they stuck labels on the bags, I heard the voice of Mother - who had walked down to the garage in dressing gown and boots.

"And where were you last night Officer?" said Mum scathingly. "When next door's field was swarming with drug addicts?" Under Mothers glare both policemen turned a bright shade of pink. "Geoff's car has never moved for weeks, and the only thing I can see on the seats is dog hair. I'm glad this sort of thing doesn't happen in Seville ... I don't know what's happened to Yorkshire."

After the red faced policemen left there was another knock, this time in the form of Carlton - he held a petition.

"Londoner's land rover drove up and down track all bloody night. Never slept a wink, noise sounded like bedlam. Heard about stabbing outside grave yard? Police are calling it attempted murder - some poor sod stabbed in neck, he's on life support. And that's not all- Bert behind bar had to move a suspicious car on, parked outside pub it were, looked just like Geoff's. Up to something they were, selling packets of powder that looked like sugar. You should have seen money changing hands. Bert said, 'must be dealers from city, been given a calling card. Hippies have seen to that...'"

"The accents weren't local Carlton," Mother chimed in. "I know a London twang when I hear it."

"You're an intelligent woman Evelyn, mores the pity tha not staying…"

# 21. 'I give to you all that I know'

*01.01. 1981.*

At nine forty five a.m. Geoff drove Mum to the airport. The roads were covered in black ice with visibility almost zero. He claimed my driving skills were inadequate for the conditions, so I nodded and said 'maybe they are,' but really it's my emotional skills in saying goodbye that I worry about. I know I will miss mother every minute of every day until her charisma gradually lessens. So, after saying goodbye, I handed the airport run over to Geoff. When she left, everywhere felt dull and empty. Life had lost its sparkle. The glamour had gone, and now everything seemed tedious. Even Shelly wore a sad expression.

"Your Mum is one of those special people who radiate happiness all around her." Shelly filled yet another wheelbarrow with muck and sighed. "Can you hear the tribe in the next field strolling up to the Pub for breakfast? Thank goodness I slept through the turmoil."

"But you're in a back bedroom, and you had 'sounds of the ocean' playing all night. I could hear the dolphins whistling."

"The sound's so calming … it sends me to sleep. Before I came here I used to suffer from insomnia, but not now. All this fresh air followed by sounds of the sea just knocks me out," she said dreamily. "But I think Ganador must have been disturbed by the din, he's quieter than usual."

"Maybe he's missing mum."

"Your mum had a natter with Ganador every morning- she brought him cups of tea with sugar lumps and thoroughly spoiled

179

him. Evelyn has a magical effect on every living thing she passes by. I'm missing her already…"

In the afternoon Geoff went down to the yard to exercise the waiting horses, 'stretch their legs,' he said, 'had too many days off over Christmas and so have I."

As he placed his foot in the stirrup I suddenly realized that something was not quite right, something different was happening. The something different was Ganador's tranquility, he stood still as a statue for Geoff to mount, without one step of piaffe.

"Is he coming down with something?" I queried, and Geoff dismounted to search for his thermometer. He knew I would only worry if he did nothing … a change in behavior often signaled a raised temperature.

"I suppose it never does any harm to check." He stared at the mercury pretending to look surprised at the level. "Perfectly normal," he said. "The lad's becoming single minded, more able to concentrate. Perhaps it's his New Year resolution…" After straightening the stirrup leathers, he adjusted his cap and tightened the girth before leading him over to the mounting block. Geoff always carried out the same three checks before riding.

"It's not his physical health," Shelly said knowingly. "He could be pining for Evelyn, or perhaps he's worried? Hope he doesn't think I'm about to 'do a Sue on him.' Can't understand people coming and going can you Lad?" She rubbed Ganador's nose and plaited his forelock. "Yesterday, he caught sight of my weekend case and his big black eyes stood out on stalks. I'm sure he followed it all the way across the yard." Shelly was extremely convincing, her views on just about anything rang out like statements of fact, and somehow, she always sounded believable.

"And what's 'to do a Sue' mean? Is it a new Americanism?" Living on top of the moors had the disadvantage of never hearing new expressions, present day novelties of speech passed me by, as did daily papers. I was lodged in the past with the farmers, may as well admit it.

"Walk out and leave him of course!" Shelly was never anything but strong minded; her thought process didn't bend, amend, or change direction. "David the vet once told me that horses are far more sensitive than any human, he said they feel pain three times more than we do, hear underground streams we never knew existed- and even feel their rider's stress! 'If you feel irritable don't ride' he said, 'wasting your time.' And did you know a horse has a better memory than an elephant? And elephants never forget..."

"But only days ago," I reminded her, "Ganador hadn't changed at all, chased a hiker up the footpath, jumped a five barred gate twice, and passaged round the yard. Only days ago, he was his usual boisterous- battling- self..."

"Therefore," said Shelly, with conclusive finality, "he's pining for your Mum."

Geoff had long since turned his attention to Ganador, who for once looked to be concentrating on his rider. I knew that Geoff would take advantage of his calmer state of mind for just as long as was possible. For a time, I watched the pair in the school. Ganador's paces were effortless. In movement he became magnificent, an elegant poise in his every stride, relaxed power in every line of his body. No matter how many times I saw him, Ganador always stirred a deep emotion within me. The kind of feeling that had long lain undisturbed in some corner of my mind and which I didn't fully understand.

The work other horses found difficult, or even impossible, seemed simple to Ganador, as simple as breathing. Raking the sand after Ganadors exercise was barely necessary for his movement was of the air just as equally as the ground. His favored airs were of piaffe and passage, which he performed with outstanding bravura.

Until that moment in the school I had not realized how correct the words of Fernando were to prove, Ganador was a miracle of equine creation an exact replica of his forefathers, the Battle Horse of King's. What an awesome sight they must have been, galloping into combat, fierce, invincible, the most wanted battle horse in Europe ... and the most beautiful.

After watching Ganador, I walked down to the stables to start changing the horse's rugs for the cold night ahead. Already, darkness had fallen with its sub zero temperatures and blustery winds blowing off the moor, it was the kind of cold only felt in high places, stabbing.

Once in the tack room I neatly folded the day rugs, tidied up and removed Fernando's letter from the second drawer of the display cabinet. There was something comforting about the tack room with its smells of shoeing and newly cleaned leather. It was a place where no one disturbed me, where I brought orchestral scores or books to read, sitting warmly wrapped in horse blankets.

Following turning off the bright yard lights, I sat under the single bulb to re read the letter. As I read, the beauty of Fernando's prose flowed over me; his knowledge answered my every question. The instant I came to his last word, I immediately wanted to read it again and again. He evoked threads of understanding that connected me to Ganador's way of thinking, clues that allowed me to get under his skin. There's one passage I can't take my eyes away from, its words are so very powerful. I start to copy it into my diary hoping that some of what I write will stay in my mind forever.

*'The pure Spanish horse is rarely kalm again when abused; therefore Ganador can never give to you all that he wishes. If you treat him kindly though firmly and with respect, show much patience but never any anger he may decide to trust you a little. Always remember you have time to be all these things.*

*I have been at pains to point out that Ganador will find highly collected work much easier. The royal line was bred to display ability in High School; Ganador is a King a noble battle horse. Born in a century when his attributes are no longer required. Long ago his ability to fly through the air and his great courage revealed supremacy. Today these same characteristics are regarded by many as a secondary branch of the Arab horse. Who wants a horse that possesses fighting spirit, a horse who flies through the air, wishing only to carry his master into battle? The exercises of High*

*School are in his blood, the same exercises that once made the Iberian horse famous.'*

With the first message were two envelopes, training programs for February and March. The first was headed 'work on two tracks,' the second 'minus plus ultra.' Tomorrow, I will seal the letter and put it in the post box for Michelle to discover. Later in the week Geoff will find the letter, he will delve in and out the way he does, saying it sounds more like poetry than training advice.

\*

That evening I rang Mum, "I had a wonderful Christmas," she said. "I'll always have a story to tell my friends, such a lot happened ... and I thought it was quiet on the moors, couldn't have been more wrong!" When I read Fernando's letter out, she sounded very impressed. "Do you know Norma, it reads like poetry. Fernando has artistry, plus a vast knowledge of his subject. I remember your Dad mentioning him." We were both silent for a moment, there was something not quite right in saying 'dad' ... not yet. Mum breathed deeply and struggled on. "He used to call such writing, the language of wisdom. Is Fernando a Portuguese grand master?" she asked, thankful to be away from her mistake. "And didn't his father save the old Iberian breed from extinction?" She had an amazing memory, remembered conversation's that had taken place years ago, word for word. Never forgot the contents of a concerto, if she liked it. Mum didn't need a score book, she could remember every note. "How's my Ganador today? Do you know, I have missed chatting to him and making him cups of tea."

"Today his mood is tranquil... Shelly thinks he's missing you. But on the work front, he seems to find collected movements so easy - exercises other horses' find difficult are effortless to Ganador. Fernando said: 'He is a King a noble battle horse. Born in a century when his attributes are no longer needed. And that the airs of High School are in his blood.'"

"What do you think?"

"His natural abilities have to be inherited, that's what I think. No-one understands Horses of King's anymore…"

"Ganador was born in the wrong century," she said. "How is it possible for people to understand?"

"Fernando told me he would love the work other horses hate, because he was bred for supremacy on the battle field. At that point in time, I found it difficult to believe, but now, I can see what he means. Every time I look at him, I imagine those fighting horses of long ago…"

"I suppose someone with Fernando's knowledge of Iberian horses and breeding has seen everything…

And before I forget, be very careful driving over to Ilkley. I know you want to go to this musical meeting, but those moorland roads strike terror into me. Do remember there's always another time." I never answered Mum, as far as I was concerned the weekend was booked- hotel, practice rooms and the plus point of tuition with a famous string quartet group. Oh no, I wasn't missing this arts council treat, not for snow, not for anything. "Give my love to everyone over there. I'll speak to you soon."

A delivery of mail arrived the following morning, the first since the blizzard. I selected three late Christmas cards, picked up Fernando's letter and carried the post into the kitchen.

"Why are you smiling on such a freezing morning?" Shelly asked cheerfully.

"A letter from Fernando," I replied placing the post on the table. "And before you ask, yes, the stamp is Portuguese." I can feel her eyes staring curiously at the package.

"Not 'the' Fernando Sue told me about in her last letter?" Shelly spent the most part of her free hours keeping in touch with friends, most of the evening in fact.

"Did I hear you say Sue?" I said disbelievingly. "Never knew you and Sue were so chummy."

"Sue and I try to keep in touch. I think she feels lonely."

"She hasn't mentioned feeling lonesome, but we plan to go over and see her next year."

"Sue asked me to send Fernando's address, together with anything I can glean from his letters. She told me his letters are far more interesting than any book. Please Norma... read a few lines then I can get back to her. Promise to pressurize Kit into painting the tack room again." So I opened the package, and read the first few lines.

*'I have found the championship Ganador won – it was the Pair Driving Championships held in Seville, together with his brother Papillon. At the time he was three years old! Perhaps the name Ganador implies this. You can be proud of his achievement, but sad he was broken as a driving horse'*

Shelly gasped, as the full implications of Ganadors famous past struck her. No doubt Sue would be informed later today or maybe even this afternoon by way of my phone.

"Just imagine; my Ganador champion of Seville! I always knew he was special; it's something in his eyes. I'm writing New Year cards tonight to everyone on my contact list and I am not keeping his famous past a secret." She was right, his eyes held a strange power, a look of supremacy, of dominance, at times they looked unyielding. "Sometimes when he stares at me, I begin to feel uneasy. It's as though he brings about a world of memories, as if, he allows me to experience his timeless world. Always, I'm aware of a strange feeling of arrogance, that 'he owes me nothing...but I owe him everything.' Do you understand me ... am I making sense?"

"Perfect sense, I've felt it myself." Who was I to scorn? I too had fallen hopelessly under Ganador's spell. "I think what you are describing is called animal wisdom, it's a power human's can't understand. A tension of two wills, the human master together with the silent animal, two extraordinary spirit's of creation..."

Whatever the future held it was my duty to care for this stallion for the rest of his earthly span. Never would I allow him to face the indignity of having to be sold, passed on yet again like an item of furniture. I possessed a passionate loyalty towards this Kingly creature and so did Geoff. The moment Michelle returned to the stables, I sat at my desk and opened the first envelope, the package intended for March: 'Minus plus ultra,' I placed in the bottom drawer.

'We have come a long way in Ganadors basic work, following careful training to strengthen his weaknesses. If and when problems arise return to an earlier part of ze training. Find where the problem has begun. If necessary return to the beginning. But please, never pressurize him until he shows resistance, never. Trust is difficult to regain, as is soundness.

*Work On Two Tracks.*

Please remember to think always of the rhythm. Also of importance is only to ask for that which he is capable of giving, comfortably and without strain. Ganador has been returned to health but he will never be capable of giving to you all that he wishes.

Always use the same regularity of rhythm between the paces and during transitions. This must be counted with precision, like clockwork. At times reward a few good strides by discontinuing the exercise and riding forwards- but in perfect rhythm, then 'otra vez' or one more time! Never continue for too long or hold him into any lateral movement with strong aids. This is not training but straining. We work towards complete lightness when ze horse finds it acceptable to obey, in perfect balance, regular rhythm using very little effort; this applies to the rider also!

Pirouettes in walk can help restore kalm if worked in perfect rhythm. Remember to maintain the rhythm in a forwards direction on coming out of this movement. Activate the pirouette as in piaffe.

Movements should only be ridden for ten to fifteen minutes but riding forwards to develop the paces thirty minutes.

*Never train without kalm, it is not possible without kalm.*
*Piaffe and Passage*
*Ganador will find collected work much easier! It is in his blood this work he was bred for.*
*Now begin to teach the collected halt from which he must always be ready to depart into trot. Then little by little reduce strides between halt and trot. Always count, even in halt and remember the collected paces must begin collected from the very first stride. Therefore prepare the transition, he must be balanced and working in rhythm with the first stride departing in the tempo required by the rider.*
*Differences within Paces.*
*The difference within the paces must be clear, from collected trot to lengthened trot, collected canter to more lengthened strides. But always finish work in collection by opening up ze trot remembering to prevent injury by riding through corners and round circles never with lengthened strides. When using the two trots, collected and medium remember this is a gymnastic of the loins, croup, hocks and fetlocks, only to be carried out in perfect balance and for short periods.*

*Sensible Preparation.*

*It is not a riding method we are following but sensible preparation, building strength and loosening the joints always without strain. Think of the human body preparing to perform as a dancer or athlete, not surprisingly dressage training is exactly the same.*
*When done with intelligence it kan be good; intelligence more than any other quality. Therefore it is important to understand gymnastics whilst thinking of the horses problems!*
*Everything kan be good when done with intelligence but dangerous when done without intelligence.*
*And so, this section comes to its end, once more repeating*

*the golden rules of classical equitation IMPULSION, STRAIGHTNESS, RHYTHM and the development of the paces, for without the golden rules we kan never show good progress.'*
*I give to you all that I know…*

As I read, then reread the words, 'I give to you all that I know…,' I felt deeply moved. Who else would share their lifetimes study and work with a mere friend? Who but Fernando, would spell out the rules behind classical training with such clarity of vision? Fernando had taught me the logic that lies behind correct training, had identified strengths and areas needing developing, always kindly and with encouragement. Without Fernando I might never have seen a pathway through chaos, never believed it may be possible to overcome mental and physical problems in a horse. Once more I read his letter … I remembered the day in Portugal when he took me aside and said:

'It is a serious offence to keep ones knowledge under lock and key. We have a duty, an obligation to freely give of our knowledge to those wishing to learn, to put the ball in their court as you say. It is for others to decide what to take from our work and what to leave behind. But always we must strive to leave the world a better place.' His tone was serious but at the same time light hearted. Fernando had put the training of Ganador on the road to becoming a very exciting adventure, with the finishing line always in sight.

Before turning off the lamp, I wrote a short thank you note. After the pleasantries, I wrote down what my heart told me to say:

'Dear learned Professor Fernando,

You, have given me all the knowledge in the world, I can never thank you enough…'

At that moment, I made a vow, a vow to share Fernando's knowledge with others. There had to be people like myself, who wished to learn the history behind the art of classical equitation, from the pen of a Portuguese Master trainer. Learn how this history was related, as it began, in the origins of the Spanish combat horse. After all, I had an obligation to freely give of my knowledge, just as

Fernando always had. I must leave the world a better place...

I gazed out, through the tiny mullioned window situated above my desk the one which looked out over the moor. To my surprise the top lamp on the farm track blurred white before the bright flashing lights of a snow plough. The moorland road would be open tomorrow. It might be possible to drive to Ilkley after all...

*'It is always necessary to learn from teachers who are masters of that particular art form. Whether it is classical equitation, music, literature or dance is immaterial. We must always search for the pure classical art and then savor it; never allowing what little is left to die.'*

*Fernando*

# 22. 'Land Rovers can't fly?'

*Diary, Ilkley, January 4.*

*'What have I learned after two days in Ilkley? That I can't wait to get back to Geoff and the horses, and that string quartet playing is the most testing art form going. There's no mask, no one to hide behind, and no conductor to blame. Each player is a soloist yet completely dependent on the other three. When, we just happened to find balance. When that equilibrium occurred, there was nowhere nearer heaven than the glorious sound of four counterpoints in flawlessly ordered rhythm and harmony. This weekend has been awesome...'*

After dropping Mary off in Burnley, I drove towards Cliviger, a pretty Lancashire village standing on the edge of the moors. The Christmas lights were sparkling at the Kettledrum Inn and sounds of jazz drifted on the still night air. I pulled into the side, switched off the engine and allowed the familiar music to bring back memories. The melody was 'Gershwin's summertime', dad's favorite song. Whenever he heard the opening bars, he would sigh and say 'the song that conquered the world.' It had been playing on that magical night in Jerez, the night of his last birthday. After the music ended I sat listening to the comforting hum of voices, not really wanting to break the spell. Before I drove away I checked the time ... it was after nine thirty, so much had happened in the past two days that my sense of time had gone missing, I'd become disconnected from reality. But now I longed to get back home to Geoff, the farm and the horses. To the world I loved.

Turning sharp left, I followed the winding road through the village. Past brightly lit cottages with fairy lights in trees, homes where proper people lived, homes that stood on the boundary of the moors. Where the copse ended and the trees withered away, I entered the darkness of the moorland road. A transition that felt like crossing between two worlds, a world that lived, and one left abandoned ... untarnished by the wants of man. Or as Geoff once said, 'an empty wilderness, and better for it...'

As I drove higher, the temperature plunged to biting cold. Tall banks of frozen snow sparkled at either side of the road, just like a scene from the North Pole, often higher than the land rover roof. I sighed with relief as I drew away from the walls of snow and saw the open moors. Stopping, I wrapped a fur shawl around my ears, buried my fingers in sheepskin gloves and placed a blanket across my knees. Shivering with relief, I began to feel warmer. Energy returned, I gazed at the surrounding wilderness. As far as I could see, the moor shimmered in a covering of ice. Above the horizon, a flame of orange gold lit up the heavens, the kind only seen on moonless nights. To the south, a line of stark black hills stood etched into the night sky, rock solid and constant. I loved the hills.

Before the bends I went through the usual checks, automatic by now, impossible to forget... dip headlights, into second gear, reduce speed to crawling pace. In the distance I saw lights flashing, probably a car pulling out of the shooting club. The lights gathered speed. Horrified, I watched a car accelerate towards me- it was in the middle of the road- I tried to stop. The land rover rocked as the car thundered past ... and then my world went mad.

I felt a wrench as a wheel hit something solid- the steering wheel kicked out of my hands. I watched it spinning like a top as the land rover did its own thing and climbed the roadside wall. Briefly it stopped and lurched. I remember looking into blackness, feeling disconnected from the chaos around me ... and then it fell with a crash. When the metal stopped groaning I tried to work out where I was. Closing my eyes, I saw black. When I opened them nothing had changed, except for an ominous dripping sound from the engine.

'Turn the engine off'- said my inner voice. But the keys were gone, disappeared in the blackness.

'You have to get out'- But how?

'Through the backdoor'- The dog guards in the way.

'Loosen fittings'- I tore at the fastenings until I could squeeze underneath, crawling to what must be the backdoor and freedom. I reached for the handle, it refused to budge. With my fists I pounded on the door feeling fury and panic both at the same time.

'You have to rest'- The effort of movement in my upside down topsy turvy world exhausted me.

'Unfasten dog guard use as ladder'- Somehow, I did just that. Dragging the metal guard over to the steering wheel I hoisted it up to what might be the passenger door. After climbing up the rungs I searched for the handle, but working out where it was and which way to pull ... seemed impossible.

'How can I think when everything is upside down?' After figuring out how to open the door I realized there was no chance. The weight of a land rover door when above my head was immovable. 'Why had I not thought?'

'There's an iron bar in the back'- I want to give up ... to close my eyes and drift away. Sod the iron bar.

'You can do it'- For a few minutes I stood very still on that metal guard, too tired to move. Then I went through the whole wretched process again. I found the metal bar, climbed the guard and tried to wedge it through the door opening. I pushed my arms through, then my upper body. My first breath of fresh air was nothing short of a miracle.

'One last shove'- And the door swung back. Heaving my body onto the door frame, I sat in darkness staring at the side of what must be a hill... and crying tears of joy.

'You have to jump'- With eyes tightly closed I released my grip and jumped... waiting to be hurt.

'Your lucky day'- Amazingly, I'd landed on snow covered undergrowth, my only blemish a bleeding arm. When I sat up I gazed at the night sky, it looked wonderful. For a while I sat completely still, stunned by the beauty of everything around me. Surrounded by rocks, boulders, and snow, such mundane objects, but possessing the magic of diamonds…

When better able to balance, I found my way to the demolished wall. Using this as a guide I walked to the nearest roadside farm. Almost immediately I saw a glow, maybe it was a dwelling. Light shone dimly from its windows, a cobblestone path led to its door. Feeling thankful I'd found somewhere, I went up to the door and hammered with my fists. A man with a ginger beard and copper colored hair opened the door, I was sure I recognized him. He said: 'Hi, what a surprise.' He led the way into his kitchen, all the while listening to my story. Placing a cup of tea on the table, he said, 'Drink this…' and went about cleaning up my arm.

"Do you remember where you've been?" he asked.

After thinking hard I had to say 'No.'

"Any bump to the head region?"

"Not that I know of…"

"Don't worry," the man said kindly, "it's just shock. You're minds still fixed in forward mode … some call it survival instinct. Another cup of sweet tea might help."

After the sugary drink I began to remember places and conversations from the past two days. How had I forgotten I was driving back from Ilkley? With a jolt, I suddenly remembered packing away my violin case in the back of the land rover, before driving away from the hotel.

"I have to go back," I said abruptly, "my violins in the back." Standing up I headed for the door. He held my arm. I tried to pull away.

"Follow me," the man said. Grabbing his torch he led the way into the inky darkness of the moorland road. We found my land rover behind a partly demolished, ice covered wall, it lay on its side in a ditch. In the stillness, I heard the sound of drips from its engine, the smell of fuel brought back the terror of being trapped inside, chilling, unnerving …

"Did you turn the engine off?" He never waited for an answer.

Jumping down into the gully he forced the back door. Crawling inside he pulled out my violin. Back in the warmth of his kitchen he made yet more sweet tea.

"You're the girl who rides the Spanish horse," he said. "I'm called Jav," he waited for my reply.

"The horse is called Ganador," I replied. "And how do you know his breed?" I tried hard to remember where I'd met him, seen him, spoken to him. How had I forgotten I'd met him, forgotten where I'd been? Once again I wanted to ask him the same question, the one I remembered from long ago. My mind felt programmed … locked. I closed my eyes and fought to think. Echoes of the first time I'd said these words raced through my mind. Then I remembered, thank God the threads of memory began to unlock. I'd seen him at the top of a hill looking down over Todmorden valley, he'd said: 'caught you dreaming'. Remembering where I'd met him made me happy. Thinking clearly, felt like breaking out of murkiness into light.

"It could be that fancy brand on his flank, or then again, it could be his God like charisma," he paused and smiled. "But the truth is, I know he's Spanish because I was born in Galicia, lived on a Yeguada." He opened a cupboard and cut two slices of cake. Placing a piece on the table he ordered me to eat. "My families still out there. Dad runs a ranch taking holiday makers out on pleasure rides. Moonlight escapades, beach parties, that sort of thing. It keeps the horses and feeds the family, can't ask for more."

Listening to his chatter calmed me. "How do you feel?" he suddenly asked.

"As if a veils lifting from my mind"

"You're coming out of shock," he said happily. "Doing just fine…"

"Why do you live out here?" I asked. "Are you a sheep farmer?"

"No way!" he laughed, he seemed somewhat taken aback. "I prefer a more eccentric lifestyle."

"Why live out here if you don't farm?"

"I'm building a boat, my friend Dan's helping. We plan to sail round the world."

"Can I see it?"

"You shouldn't be walking about."

He went across the room to the back door and out into the yard. I followed him. At the back of the farm the yard looked down over a sweeping valley. In the distance, lights sparkled from far away dwellings set in and amongst the hills.

"Can I see water?" Ripples of tremulous gold danced on what looked to be a lake.

"Could it be a reservoir?" he asked, all the time watching my reaction. "It's a picture by moonlight."

The fierce beam from a spotlight lit up a huge structure resting inside a wooden cradle. I felt overawed by its size.

"Is it supposed to look like Noah's ark?" He laughed and switched on yet another light. I watched him walk under the prow of the boat, under wood that was carved and fluted just like a painting of an ancient sailing craft. "I guess, you must be the master craftsman?"

"What do you think?" he played with my question, answering with his own.

"I think you're brilliant, I really do…" Jav opened a small door off the farm yard, it led into his workshop. He turned on a light.

"Come and look," he held the door open. I walked in. What I saw was nothing less than wonderment. This was not any old work shop, this was home to a collection of guitars … and yes, violins. There were two violins hung on its walls, instrumental body parts lay on a bench waiting to come to life, some covered with velvet cloths.

"To pass the time, earn a few pennies…" he said in a matter of fact way.

"Where did you learn?"

"Sevilla, with a guitar maker, he was brilliant."

"And now you make violins too?" I walked over to where the unfinished violins lay and stroked intricately carved scrolls.

"The sealer should be hard by now," he said gently. I pulled my hand away.

"Sorry…hope I've not moved anything."

"No," he said, "your touch is too gentle."


"My first two…" he pointed to the violins hanging on the wall. "Perhaps number three is better." Under the light, his violins shone the color of rich beeswax. Reaching out I ran my fingers over the wood.

"You're an artist," I said, meaning every word.

"Not really," he answered. "It's the playing and the value placed on the music that matters." There he goes again, ahead of any question, always puzzling. At that moment, I knew why this man had risked his life to rescue my violin. To him a violin was a highly charged living entity … complete with a soul.

"I use Scottish wood," he said. "The sound is strong yet sweet."

"Like a Stradivari?" he laughed.

"Not quite. The tonal quality is good on higher strings, poor to mediocre on lower. Can't seem to get it right…" Looking at his watch he said: "Time for another drink of sweet tea."

As he closed the door, light from his torch fell onto a wooden name plate. Painted in bold black letters on a large white board were the words,


'*WILLY FOX FARM*' At each corner of the board was a painting of a fox cub; four pairs of eyes gleamed in the dark of the night.

"Like it?" His voice brought me back to the present. "I painted the sign yesterday. Hope it says everything about Willy."

"If Willy's looking down he'll be smiling." I felt tears running down my cheeks.

"So you knew him - A clever man according to Carlton."

"Willy lived in the gorge below my farm, he cared for injured foxes."

"Read underneath…" He directed the glow from his torch onto some smaller print. When my eyes adjusted to the light I read these words…

'No Better Man Ever Set Foot on Yorkshire's Moors.'

More fragments of words, scenes, and conversations began flooding back, slipping into place in some corner of my mind. Again I fought to remember where I'd heard the words. As if by magic I recalled a night in the Shepherd at Christmas, as if in a dream, I saw Bert straighten up from his crouched position over the pumps, to call out: 'What's this ere farm called Carlton?' Before replying Carlton's face turned a bright shade of pink, he was cornered and had no choice but to reply.

'It's called Willy Fox Farm.' I remembered his every word, his flushed expression, right down to the bright blue color of his tie. The memory faded away with Bert shouting: 'Tribute to Willy Fox Lad's, drinks on house.' I thought of how the farmer's had raised their glasses, and called out:

'No better man ever set foot on Yorkshire's moors...'

"So this is Carlton's second farm, the one with moorland grazing rights?"

"It's the one he bought with help from above..." he said with a smile. And I recalled the stack of cash Willy left behind, to be shared between his friends.

"So you like it out here?"

"Living here is the best thing I've ever done."

"Where did you live before here?"

"I used to live in Manchester, hated the place. In the city, every day was a nightmare, surrounded by neighbors and stupid rules. They stopped me building my boat, claimed it prevented access to light."

"So you built the boat at home ... You had a large garden?"

"No," he said defensively, "only a small lawn. That could be why I like it out here ... no one complains anymore."

When Carlton arrived in his towing truck, more of the roadside wall had to be demolished.

"What dost tha think o bachelor pad?" Carlton nodded towards Jav's place, and then beamed a satisfied smile. "Tha can tell Evelyn she's welcome anytime. Money spinner it is," he said proudly. "Grazing rights as far as tha can see." Lifting his stick, he pointed over valley and moor. "Silas pays rent for Lad. I'm content having more land, extra sheep down ere mean extra cash from ministry." He attached a towing chain to my land rover and switched on a noisy winch. Slowly, with screams of agony the land rover was hoisted out of the ditch, across a stone edge, and onto the road... where it was shoved and pulled back to normality. Once more it stood on four wheels, with the addition of several hundred dents.

"Not come off too badly, considering..." I remarked to Carlton.

"Can't tell Lass, unless thav radar eyes. Need to see it in daylight before reaching any judgments."

"Carlton...where's Geoff?"

"All's not been smooth sailing oer at your place. Walker collapsed on footpath this morning." I can't remember asking, 'when, how, or what happened,' for I put morning and walker together and thought of Ganador and the footpath. Geoff cleaned his box out on Sunday mornings, turned Ganador out on his paddock.

"But there's a new fence between Ganador's paddock and the footpath."

"I know Lass; oss didn't touch him, just galloped oer to see what were going on. Or so t'other hiker's said. Lads dealing with police now - be ere shortly."

When Geoff arrived he took the spare key off his ring, started the engine, and said:

"Has Carlton told you?"

"Yes... I never should have gone."

"Snowed again last night, not a lot, but enough to need a snow plough in front of the ambulance."

"Carlton said there were other hiker's..."

"Yes, thank goodness we have witnesses."

Geoff turned to Carlton and said: "Lad passed away... hospital said over exertion and exposure."

"Walker's should be banned from moor in winter. He's second to meet his end in as many weeks," replied Carlton angrily.

Carlton's anger must have been catching, as Geoff walked over to look at my crashed land rover he gave the impression of being angry too: "How did this happen? Land rovers can't climb walls. Were you driving too fast for the conditions?" I never answered, just gave him a sad smile. All this was my own doing. Mum was right; I should never have left the farm in risky weather. Like a fool, I'd put everyone to a lot of trouble and almost lost my life - and for what? Arts council treats? Mum's words kept appearing out of nowhere: 'there's always another time.' Thank goodness she didn't know, didn't know what a fool I'd been. No one would believe the real story, for as Carlton so rightly said, 'land rovers can't fly.'

After thanking Jav I climbed in, sat on my seat and reached down to the pedals. Such simple things as sitting upright, having doors that opened and closed felt nothing short of amazing, having my violin safely by my side, a miracle. On reaching the safety of home, something deep inside snapped. Any previous calm I'd felt, suddenly went away and erupted into hysterical tremors, right there on the doorstep. I remember sitting by the fire desperately trying to stem the flow of tears, but to no avail.

"Straight to bed," ordered Geoff. "I'll bring milk and toast. Things always seem better in the morning."

"Maybe they do…" I said before falling asleep.

After lunch the following day, I walked down to the stables just to sit in the tack room and listen to the calming sounds of horses. Compared to my usual self, I felt like a switched off light, sad and drained.

"You can't expect to feel the same as before, at least not immediately," said Geoff from the doorway to his forge. "Effects of shock take time to heal."

"I don't understand. Last night I felt fine." Geoff raised his eyebrows, resting the shoe he was forging on the anvils face.

"Last night you were in the fast lane." He used his words carefully as though spelling out something known to him and not me. "But today the escalator rides stopped. Takes time to stop running. It's called consequences… "

*

Jav rang this morning, wanting to know how I was. After the well-mannered preliminaries of phone-line speech, he said: "Before you go, I've a favor to ask," he sounded uncomfortable about something. "We are holding our first sweat lodge ceremony next week, having it in the barn."

"Whatever's a sweat lodge?"

"It's a native Indian purification ceremony, it's very spiritual."

'Not interested,' I wanted to say. But something stopped me. I desperately wanted to please this man.

"Will you bring the Spanish horse down; just to give it an air of authenticity?" Please think about it."

"I'll do more than think about it. What time is he on show...?"

When Shelly walked in, I told her the story. How kind he'd been and how he'd saved my violin.

"Is he a hippy?"

"I suppose he is, in a far-flung way. And you know Geoff's thoughts on hippies. But I can't let him down, not after all his help."

"Stop worrying..." she replied. "Leave everything in my capable hands - and Geoff's of course. If you feel up to it come along for the ride."

On the night of Jav's ceremony, Ganador looked splendid in his Indian headdress and so did Shelly in hers. On his neck Shelly had arranged transfers of Indian faces and stern looking Chiefs, across his back hung two Moroccan saddle bags with tassels and bells. Geoff offered to drive the box down, on the condition there was to be no riding, or 'messing about,' so in the end everything worked out.

Inside the large barn, the event swarmed with strangely attired London hippies and Manchester mods, but it was really Ganador who stole the show with his many tricks and other worldly glamour. The guests all crammed into the barn, waiting their turn to sweat until pure, sitting cross legged in square shaped tents, lined with hot rocks. Inside these structures, the temperature rose to an average of one hundred and two degrees Fahrenheit, enough to melt the icicles hanging on the barn roof.

Geoff sat with Carlton in Willy Fox Farm, drinking tea and

looking out over the valley. Distant lights sparkled on and off from far away dwellings, looking down felt just like sitting in a plane en route to another land.

"I wonder what Willy would say?" asked Geoff.

"He'd say thav done right Lad. Thav spent money wisely. That's what he'd say…"

A few days after Jav's ceremony, the consequences revealed themselves. It was the first time I'd driven since the accident. The route, I knew well, straight down the main road and through Hebden Bridge, with Geoff sitting in the passenger seat.

"Turn off here," he said. "Look out for a feed mill sign, its top left."

On turning into the side street I began to panic, something I never did. The street was normal for the area, nothing unusual. Steep and narrow, the kind where terraced houses loomed oppressively at either side. Before I could gather my thoughts together, a white delivery van turned into the street from the top… it came towards me, and I flipped. Swerving right, I veered across the road and slammed into the curb.

"What the hell are you doing?" shouted a worried Geoff.

"I don't know," I snapped. "Except that I'm not driving."

Leaving the wheel in Geoff's capable hands, I walked slowly round to the passenger side. "Can't erase the accident from my mind, not yet…"

Jav came to the farm a few days later, he handed me a card, an invitation to his 'boat naming and trial launch.' On the day of the ceremony we stood behind 'Willy Fox Farm' on the valley side of the road, close to the reservoir. The guests wanted everything finished and done with quickly, so the launch came first. Here, and for some unknown reason, the boat took in water, which meant returning the splendid craft to its wooden cradle that stood in the farm yard overlooking the valley. The naming took place in Willy Fox Farm. I watched him pull a sheet of paper out of a drawer, never imagining his words would be with me for the rest of my life…

*'I name this ship Ganadora.*
*May the Divine Majesty of the southerly wind,*
*Bless all who sail in her.'*

In the following weeks of midwinter the two men gained fame in the region of North Yorkshire, not for Indian purification ceremonies, but for their skill in the carving of wood and excellent joinery. We became good friends with the bohemian craftsmen. Gradually, old doors were replaced with fine new ones, and quality fitted cupboards took the place of rickety tables. All in wood the color of rich beeswax.

I like to believe Jav's skill in the crafting of musical instruments went on to enrich many lives, helping musicians explore the endless possibilities of musical sound, where, maybe they found splendor in simple melody...

# 23. Last blizzard of winter

*Diary, February 24. 1981.*

*'Following two days of freezing cold, the temperature last night dropped to its lowest ever in sixteen years ... minus twenty in the outdoor porch. There's no wind, not even the rushes move. The moor waits for nature's wrath to come its way: still, murky dark, and so cold the air stings like needles...'*

A blizzard swept the moor on day four, with a wind so violent we fought to be heard above its screams. As the storm gained momentum, Geoff barricaded the stable doors with heavy planks and nailed plastic sheeting inside the mullioned windows.

I heard a voice say, 'better hole up until the blizzard blows itself out,' but I only heard the outer shell of someone's words - the screaming wind took the inside away. After preparing for the siege, we warmed our frozen bodies by the stove, drank coffee with spoonfuls of whisky, and took turns to poke the fire. It was then the house felt to shudder, the electric went off and the water stopped.

'Either the moors moved under our feet or the winds changed direction,' muttered Geoff. 'Due North means we're in for a bad one.'

Again, we dressed in our warmest clothes. Heads and faces covered in balaclavas, on top went Russian fur hats with ear flaps, fingers crammed into at least two pairs of gloves. Anything and everything was added, layer upon layer, to keep the driving snow away from faces and hands. Exposed skin would be bitten into by freezing ice projectiles, travelling in gusts of more than forty miles per hour.

Geoff brought oil lamps from the tack room, and stacked enough logs to feed the fire for two days. Shelly carried water from the well, whilst I held a tie rope round her waist, never moving from the farms walls. By now, there was no vision; the world had disappeared into a thick, frenzied force of snow and ice.

That night we stayed in the warm sitting room, trying to play cards under the glow of lanterns and flames from the fire. The noise of piercing screams and creaks made sleep impossible. I imagined the very structure of the house might move as eerie sounds echoed down the chimney and whirled round passageways.

'Must have lost a few roof tiles,' explained Geoff. 'The winds got into the loft...But I think we're over the worst.'

Towards morning I heard more clattering and banging, as stone roof tiles, sheds, even a barn door flew across the yard. Seized and carried away on the frenzied wind, sent spinning past the porch, until collision with a fence or wall finished their brief escapade. Left behind would be enough debris to build a bonfire, strewn over fields, twisted and crushed … just like paper.

'Winds changed direction again.' Geoff sounded happier now. 'It's hitting the corners, veering North-West, maybe losing force.'

Distant howls, slowly took the place of piercing screams. At last I was able to breathe more easily as the air pressure stabilized and the blizzard drew away. Just before eight a.m. the electric came on. Geoff cooked breakfast; it was bacon and eggs with mugs of sweet tea. We stood at the window watching snow falling in thick layers. A sense of peace had returned to the valley, and Shelly smiled for the first time in almost four days.

'This is magic' she purred. 'Who needs winter holidays, when the Austrian Alps are outside?'

A new world of startling white began to emerge from the gloom. The advancing light of day burned tiny holes through the dimness, and in the valley I gazed at a mirage of snow sweeps, stretching unbroken all the way into infinity. When the clouds dispersed, I looked at a sky of liquid red, rising above the hills, casting shafts of a rosy hue over gleaming snow.

'An image of a dream,' I thought, spellbound by the brilliance. 'Every passing picture of nature can only happen here, where the hills meet the clouds.' And I felt a twinge of grief for those who would never know such beauty…

And then my dreaming stopped … shattered by three knocks on a window pane.

"Carlton's here early. I wonder why?"

"Electrics must be off on the moor. Can't think why he likes living out there." I watched his fuzzy figure walk past the row of mullions. He walked slower than was usual; the only sound the crunch of boots on new snow. In the porch I listened to the familiar sounds of stamping of feet, brushing snow off clothes, but I never heard his signature tune…the rhythm he always rapped out with his stick.

"Can I come in," his voice had lost its usual chirpiness, he sounded forlorn.

"Sit yourself down Carlton." Shelly drew a chair close to the fire and plumped a cushion for his back. "You're frozen through man." He looked pinched with cold.

I carried in his pint mug of tea and placed it on the hearth. "Geoff's out in the yard," I said, "digging paths, feeding horses." And then he spoke.

"Mother passed away last night," he said hoarsely. Carlton covered his eyes with his cap. "Blizzard killed her…" I held his freezing hand, hoping he might feel some comfort. "She never felt safe away from village."

"You weren't to know…"

"Lass started feeling ill just before blizzard started…had to lie down she did." He sighed before continuing. "Track were impassable by then, ambulance got stuck oer Heptonstall way and police gave up on Steep's".

"And then the electric went off," I added gently, remembering last night's power cut.

"Passed away by candlelight she did, ever so peaceful in end.

Mother always said moor would finish her off. And she were right..."

*

At ten a.m. Carlton and Geoff set out across the snow covered wilderness. Geoff would hike over to Heptonstall village...and gather together 'some decent clothes for the burial, black dress, clean underwear, woolen cardigan and family bible.' Carlton would trudge up the snow filled track, back to his moorland farm, where he would sit by his mother's side for what might be the final time.

Later that afternoon, Geoff returned. He carried a cardboard box, ever so carefully. The way he held it, not too tight but carefully balanced, left nothing to my imagination.

"If the contents are alive, we're full up." He opened the lid, just enough to see inside the dark box. A snow white cat with eyes as big as saucers stared back.

"Carlton's mother's cat," he said hopefully. "It's a Persian. If you like, the cat could live in the stables. Don't want it to be a nuisance."

"No, the cat can live here. A Persian cat doesn't belong in stables ... too damp and cold." Just as I opened the box, the cat jumped out. Sedately, it walked round the room, sniffing furniture legs, looking for a cozy spot. Then it saw the object of its dreams ... a velvet cushion, where it curled up, purring contentedly.

"I couldn't leave it in the empty house..."

"Neither could I...Tell me, did the ambulance get through?"

"With the help of a snow plough, the police got there. Everything's sorted," he almost whispered. "He changed her clothes. No help in a blizzard."

For the first time in sixteen years, I heard a note of uncertainty in his voice. Cracks were appearing in my enchanted world, cracks that might widen ... until the vision of my world melted away. So I said words I never intended to speak...words that hurt.

"Promise me, we can always live here..."

"Living on top of the moors might prove impossible at some

time in the future. Nothing lasts forever."

"What will happen to the horses, or had you forgotten?"

"Have to find a farm in the valley with stables…"

"And fields and tracks to ride out on - which could take years."

"Something may turn up."

"I love this farm…I don't ever want to leave…"

I walked over to the piano opened the leather bound edition of Chopin's Nocturnes and began to play the Nocturne in Db major…the one nearest the music of angels, the nocturne I intended to perform in March, the music of the night that silenced the blackbirds with its other worldly beauty. "I love everything about this farm…" There was nothing left to say. Geoff had already made the decision. Life would become harder and increasingly perilous as each year passed. There was no arguing with the truth, moorland winters were cruel.

On holding down the final chord, I felt close to tears, the music without my knowing it, had revealed my deepest emotions with a clarity and truth that language cannot begin to name. Maybe the same insight had occurred to Geoff? Placing his hand on my shoulder he said: 'but I think we can still battle through a few more blizzards yet.' Feeling a vast wave of relief flooding over me, I turned and hugged him.

"What's that for?"

"Because you said we're staying!"

That night I sat at my desk for longer than was usual, thinking of the people who had made this journey with Ganador possible. First I wrote down Geoff. Never had Geoff failed to show bravery and patience in dangerous situations. Bravery and patience, such misunderstood words, and the only qualities that the stallion understood and respected. After all, no trainer takes kindly to the daily warfare that Ganador brought along, struggles which were sometimes of the suicidal variety. Following Geoff, I wrote Fernando … my mentor and professor. Fernando had outlined the philosophy and rules behind correct classical training, had taught me to understand Ganador's strengths and pointed out areas needing developing, always kindly and with encouragement.

As Fernando once said, 'I give to you all that I know.' And you have Fernando ... you have given me all the knowledge in the world. I can never thank you enough. After Fernando I thought of Manuel, the most exciting rider and trainer I had ever seen, and the brilliant classical trainer Nuno Oliveira, both men having formed a catalyst that would always shine within my imagination.

'Hey', a little voice whispered in my ear, 'remember my grooms.' And I remembered the grooms, who dedicated every living moment to the welfare of my horses. Life without a first class groom would be impossible to contemplate. After the grooms I thought of David the vet, always prepared to give of his expertise, whatever the weather or time.

Before I turned off the lamp I thought of Ganador, ready to start on the third phase of training, the most exciting adventure of all ... the movements of high school. At last I saw a light through the chaos that had been, it may only be fleeting, but so is everything in life. Ganador was ready to be trained in the movements that made the Iberian horse famous, exercises that seemed as natural to Ganador as breathing.

Geoff's threat about moving away from the high moor would be forgotten ... at least for now. Maybe in time he'd forget he ever said, 'nothing lasts forever.' The moors had claimed me. Just like Ganador had claimed me. I lived for the freedom of this lonely place, the music of blackbirds, the cries of hawks, to awaken to the earthy smell of peat.

To know the moor ... was to love it. To never let it go. I was a prisoner in its power.

And now, for the first time in sixteen glorious years, I must try to be sensible. If I should lose everything and my enchanted world disappears, then surely I might discover a new world, a new place to love...

*Cries of hawks in moonlight*
*Nights when blizzards rage*
*Shimmering rainbows after storms*
*Blurred images of rain*
*Pre dawn calls of cuckoos*
*Rich scent of earthy peat*
*Mist clouds melting into hills*
*Which image will remain?*

*'To Dream' N. Jimenez*

**End of Book two.**

# Brief Index of Equestrian Terms.

Spanish Horse... Andalusian, Carthusian, P.R. E., (Pure Raza Espanol)
Lusitano...Bred in Portugal. The Lusitano horse is now classed as a separate breed within Portugal.

Airs of the ground.
Piaffe...Rhythmical trot on the spot, appearing to mark time. In the ideal Piaffe the horses forearm should be almost horizontal to the ground, the hind legs active and slightly lowered.
Passage...A highly collected trot that appears to hover. The hind legs must step forwards under the body and the forearm should be almost horizontal.
Pirouette...Performed in canter or walk. The hind legs mark time whilst the forelegs describe the circumference, so turning around the hind legs.
Spanish Walk...The horses forelegs are raised and extended forwards in each stride of walk. Its knees must remain straight and the whole movement should appear graceful.

www.ingramcontent.com/pod-product-compliance
Lightning Source LLC
Chambersburg PA
CBHW071153260626
47162CB00003B/1027